T0308559

Suspicion

Suspicion

Laura Grimaldi

Translated by
Robin Pickering-Iazzi

THE UNIVERSITY OF WISCONSIN PRESS
TERRACE BOOKS

The University of Wisconsin Press
1930 Monroe Street
Madison, Wisconsin 53711

www.wisc.edu/wisconsinpress/

3 Henrietta Street
London WC2E 8LU, England

Originally published as *Il sospetto*
Copyright © 1989 by Laura Grimaldi
Translation copyright © 2003 by Robin Pickering-Iazzi.

1   3   5   4   2

Printed in the United States of America

Library of Congress Cataloging-in-Publication Data
Grimaldi, Laura.
[Sospetto. English]
Suspicion: a novel / Laura Grimaldi;
translated by Robin Pickering-Iazzi.
p.   cm.
ISBN 0-299-18860-4 (alk. paper)
I. Pickering-Iazzi, Robin Wynette.   II. Title.
PQ4867.R493 S6713   2003
853'.914—dc21   2003005651

Terrace Books, a division of the University of Wisconsin Press,
takes its name from the Memorial Union Terrace, located
at the University of Wisconsin–Madison. Since its inception in 1907,
the Wisconsin Union has provided a venue for students, faculty, staff,
and alumni to debate art, music, politics, and the issues of the day.
It is a place where theater, music, drama, dance, outdoor activities,
and major speakers are made available to the campus and the community.
To learn more about the Union, visit www.union.wisc.edu.

Suspicions amongst thoughts
are like bats amongst birds,
they ever fly by twilight.
Francis Bacon, *Essays*

Suspicion

I

Two things made Matilde Monterispoli suspect that she had given birth to a murderer. They occurred over the course of the same day, and though seemingly unrelated, the uneasiness that had nagged at her since morning finally became clear after what happened that night.

In the morning, she noticed that the case of scalpels was slightly out of place.

In the evening, the police were in her own home.

The case had always sat on the mantel of the austere, black-veined marble fireplace that stood in the small sitting room just off Matilde's bedroom. She had put it there herself, the day the doctors from Santo Giovanni Hospital solemnly returned it to her. They had come as a delegation to give their condolences for her husband, who had died of a heart attack while he was operating on a patient. The case was made of mottled leather, with a silver buckle, and had belonged to Matilde's father for years. He had given it to Nanni on the day of their wedding as a token for good luck in his career and also as a gesture of gratitude because he was taking that taciturn, touchy young woman off his hands.

3

~~~~~~~~~~

When the case was returned, Matilde had put it right in the middle of the fireplace mantel with the end of the buckle pointed toward an oblong black spot in the marble. Since then, no one else had ever touched it. She could not stand to have strangers in her bedroom or the sitting room. So every morning she took a yellow dust cloth out of the bottom drawer of the desk in front of the window, preferring to dust every piece of furniture and every single item herself.

Now the case was out of place, with the buckle pointing at least a couple of inches away from the tip of the spot. Matilde stood there staring at it as if it were an omen. At first it was only a feeling, or a premonition, that tortured her the entire day, even though she kept telling herself over and over again that it was wrong to let herself think such terrible things. The loneliness was undoubtedly affecting her.

Matilde lived with her son, Enea, in a house that had become too big for the two of them alone after Nanni died. It was a beautiful, sprawling two-story home in San Domenico di Fiesole, painted a soft yellow with green shutters. The house was surrounded by a deep garden that isolated it from the street and by a hedge of boxwood that had been trimmed less and less over the years and now completely screened the building from view. When Nanni was alive, they used all the rooms in the house—the bedrooms on the second floor and the study, the living and sitting rooms, and large dining room on the main floor. Afterward, Matilde moved her bedroom and Enea's downstairs and had radiators installed just on the first floor.

There was a path to the house with four cypress trees on each side leading up to two flights of steps that branched off to the right and the left and opened onto

4

a small, semicircular portico. The garden was divided into lots of kidney-shaped flower beds bordered by low stone walls and planted mostly with roses. But the most beautiful thing about the garden were the great, age-old trees. The garden was not particularly well kept, but not neglected either. There was an old man who came to pull out the weeds and fertilize the beds, and if needed, he added gravel to the path and the walkways between the flower beds. Matilde had never wanted to replace the gravel with something more permanent because for her it was like a guard dog that warned her about any unfamiliar footsteps.

That evening, though, it did not warn her about the two men who were approaching the house. If she had been in her bedroom, she would have heard it crunch under their feet, but she was at her desk in the sitting room, and the window faced the side of the house. When the doorbell rang, Matilde raised her head and listened, convinced she must have heard wrong. It had been years since she had had any visitors at her house in the evening. The doorbell rang again repeatedly and, it seemed to Matilde, insistently. At that point she got up, went into the bedroom, and looked outside, just slightly cracking the shutters. The old hinges squeaked lightly, and one of the two men turned around. "Police," he said.

Matilde pulled back from the windowsill and went to open the door. For all the time it took her to walk step by step across the bedroom and the sitting room and then down the stretch of hallway leading to the entry, it was still not enough to let her gather any thoughts. She acted automatically, without even asking herself if the two men might not really be who they said they were. She cracked the door just halfway open, keeping her body hidden behind the thick, reassuring wood and waiting for them to take the initiative. She could not have said how they managed to get into the house. One of them somehow slipped in between the door and the jamb. Just as she turned to look at him, the other one was inside too. They headed toward the sitting room, following the light.

"We need to speak with Enea Monterispoli," said the one who had come inside first. He had light brown hair with dark blond streaks and unusually restless dark eyes. "Is he a relative of yours?"

"My son," Matilde answered, motioning to indicate that at that point they might as well be seated. They remained standing. While one of them went over to the window, the other one went over to the desk and seized the household accounts that she had been going through when they arrived. He looked them over carefully, then put them down again.

Just then, Matilde was overcome by a deep sense of alarm. "What has my son done?" She immediately regretted the question, impulsively blurted out, and added, "What do you want with him?"

"Where is he?" the same policeman asked.

Matilde answered that he was not at home and she had no idea where he might be. For no reason she added, "My son is almost fifty years old." If someone had told her that in that moment she was distancing herself from Enea she would have been truly surprised.

The policemen were in their thirties. They had a couple of days growth of beard and their eyes were bloodshot. Tension seeped through their pores, spreading to Matilde.

"According to our information, Enea Monterispoli owns a gun. Where does he keep it?"

6

"I don't know anything about a gun," she lied, wondering how they could think she would betray her son. She was standing behind the small easy chair in the corner of the room, and kept herself from clenching her hands on the back of the chair.

"Tell him to show up at number 2 on via Zara by seven o'clock tomorrow evening. Homicide squad," the policeman ordered. All of a sudden he seemed to be in a hurry to leave. When she replied that surely she had a right to know something more, he answered, "You must have heard about the double homicide the other night. We need to talk with your son. It would be better for him if he didn't make us come back again." As he started to walk toward the hall he added, "Tell him to bring the gun too."

Then the second policeman spoke for the first time, and Matilde was taken aback. The man suddenly turned toward her. He looked her straight in the eye and said, "Where was your son the last few evenings? In particular, where was he on Friday?"

Matilde's hands were moist with perspiration. She wiped them on her skirt, forcing herself not to show she was afraid. "As I said, my son is almost fifty."

"Well, did he stay at home on Friday? Or did he go out? You must know that at least."

"But you see, when he's at home, my son . . ." She was about to say that her son spent the evenings in the quarters above the lemon-tree room, and stopped herself just in time. "My son sleeps at the end of the hall," and she pointed to Enea's bedroom. "It's unlikely I'd hear him."

Then the first policeman came out with a remark that left her totally astonished. "We certainly wouldn't be the ones to force a mother to betray her son." It was as if he had read her mind. Matilde suddenly felt tired and vulnerable.

After they had gone, she prepared herself to wait. Enea often came home very late, but that night she would stay up. The house was furnished with solid pieces of antique furniture, some quite valuable, that creaked and moaned during the night as if they were alive. There was a dressing table in particular, where Matilde sat every morning to fix her hair and spread a dab of cream on her face. It had a crack running across it that barely showed at first but now stood out as if it had been carved by a knife. That was where she settled in to wait for her son. That was where she connected the scalpels that had been disturbed to the two police-men's visit.

That was also where she began to deeply resent Enea, because he had dragged those two men into her home, violating it with their presence. From that night on, it would never be the same again. It was as though they had brought inside the concrete reality of fear and violence, emotions that had never crossed that thresh-old before.

2

The new moon shrouds the sky at an emergency stop on the right shoulder of the road to Certaldo, and the darkness swallows everything. Thick vegetation envelops three sides of the space where the car is parked. A steady stream of traffic flows down the main road, but the ribbons of light from the headlights do not penetrate the bushes.

The young woman is the first one to notice the large shadow take shape and move toward the car. She is in the back seat, waiting for the young man to join her. In the front seat, bending over to look for the tissues under the dashboard, he feels her fingers clawing at his hair, jerks away to get free, and something scratches his skin. He is about to say "are you crazy?" but his girlfriend's scream is so loud and piercing it fills him with fear. He sees the shadow too. He fumbles to start the car and puts it into reverse. But he forgets the hand brake, and the car moves backward, lurching in violent jumps and starts.

The shadow raises one arm, aims, and fires at the windshield. It advances quickly, moving faster than the car. It reaches the car and puts one hand on the roof while continuing to shoot with the other one, this time inside the left window. The car jerks out of the emergency stop. It cuts across the road, gives one last lurch, and winds up nose down in the ditch on the opposite side.

The young man's body violently shudders three times, as each bullet hits him. One bullet drives into the muscles of his shoulder, the other two go straight into his head. The woman is hit in the forehead, and her only movement is convulsive and involuntary. The hand clutching at the man's hair, as if seeking protection, recoils. The buckle of her watch gets tangled in his hair, the band breaks, and the watch falls on the floor mat.

The huge shadow stops, rising to a height that the flashing beams from the headlights distort and elongate, projecting it onto the darkness beyond the rays of light. It looks enormous. It slips its hand through the shattered car window, rips the keys out of the ignition, and hurls them off into the bushes. Then it shoots again, this time at the headlights, the only witnesses to the crime.

The man does not linger to viciously attack the woman's body as he did the other times. He does not take out the knife to cut his victim's soft flesh as in the previous murders.

At the fourth to the last murder, he used the knife to try it out and test its effectiveness, haphazardly piercing and slicing the body, stripped from the neck to the thighs, sinking it into the heart and the liver. When he was sure how it worked, he knelt down religiously next to the lifeless body, with his head bent down so low it almost brushed against it. His hands moved by touch in the darkness, as he made a long cut from the right temple to the lip, then down to the chin, and then still further down to the breast, following its contour. Finally down to the pubis, along the outline of pubic hair. At this point he stopped, unable to make any real sense of his motions. Then he tore off a shoot from a vine bordering the field where he had dragged the young woman, and inserted it deep into her vagina, confusedly, as though exploring the consistency and depth.

At the third to the last murder, the knife moved more rapidly, conscious of its real objective and the line to follow. With three clean cuts it removed the pubis, which the man then brandished in his gloved hand, holding it up like a trophy in the darkness of night.

At the next to the last murder, after the ritual of the gun shots—increasingly clean and precise—the knife moved without hesitation, as if it had a life of its own. It cut the flesh from the pubis to the inside of the thighs, wedging it away from the fatty layer, preparing it for the hand that was already extended, so that it could tear it out and raise it high into the sky as a sign of victory. This time the man stayed long enough to re-position the young woman's body, joining her hands on her chest in an act of obscene piety.

At the last murder, the challenge to battle is between him and the young man. As man to man. The young man dared to try to escape his attack, but he proved he was the strongest. He prevented the escape. He blocked the car and completed the slaughter. When he ripped the keys out of the dashboard and hurled them into the dark, he was swept away by a sort of delirious omnipotence that fully satisfied him, extinguishing the drive to use the knife.

꙳꙳

If she could have, Matilde would have erased the memory of the disturbed scalpels and the two policemen from her mind. Since that was impossible, she continued to wrack her brain, searching for the hidden meaning of the latest events. She had asked Enea if he had gone to the police and if he had taken the gun along, adding in a low voice that she had told those two men she did not know anything at all about a gun.

As far as it seemed, Enea had gone to the police and considered the matter cleared up. But Matilde was still worried about it. Why in the world had they looked for him of all people? They must have had some reason. The police certainly did not do things for no reason at all.

"In fact, they had a reason," replied Enea. "They're checking all of the registered guns, and Papa's gun is registered." Then he quickly changed the subject. Matilde's uneasiness did not disappear even when Enea, noticing the set expression on her face, told her again not to worry, everything was straightened out.

Right away, Matilde cautiously sounded him out about the scalpels. Was he the one who had touched them? Enea stared at her with his blue eyes for a few moments, without saying a word, and finally shook his head. That silent denial made her all the more anxious.

She broached the subject again a few nights later while they were having dinner. She led into the conversation on a general note, beginning with the unusual violence that had been rocking the city for some time.

"It doesn't really seem all that unique to me," Enea said. His tone became didactic, as it did whenever he talked with his mother. "The violence around today is just the same as before. Not because violence was born with humanity, as too many people maintain. It's that the human mind is no longer able to tolerate or resolve the tensions it's subjected to. When it reaches its limits, it can only be released through violence. If it can't be expressed collectively, it becomes individual."

In a burst of anger, Matilde's voice cracked. "Since the day I was born I have never heard of monsters that go around with a gun killing young people barely twenty years old. Not to mention the way the bodies of the young women were butchered. You can't tell me that's normal."

"No, it's not normal," said Enea, cutting the conversation short. "But since it's happening, it's possible."

After Enea had gone out one morning, Matilde felt so worried she was driven to go upstairs to the quarters above the lemon-tree room, which her son had made into a study and a woodworking shop of sorts. They called them the quarters above the lemon-tree room even though only one of the rooms was actually above the one where the pots of lemon trees were stored away from the winter cold. The other room was directly above Matilde's bedroom. Enea spent countless hours up there in the evening, reading or carving wood. Sometimes he would come home with pieces of a tree trunk or a block of wood from an olive tree, which he would lug up to the workshop to carve animals, human figures, or vases. He kept the keys hung on a hook attached to the side of the cupboard in the kitchen, but did not let anyone touch them. When Matilde told Saveria, their housekeeper, to go upstairs to check what shape Signor Enea's rooms were in, she waited for him to be at home so that he could open the door for her. Once she was inside, she quickly swept the middle of the floor, her movements hampered by the piles of books heaped in every corner of the room.

13

She dusted the table without disturbing the papers and files, and emptied the ashes from the majolica stove during the cold season. She came back downstairs muttering that it was impossible to clean that way, with Signor Enea there watching over her as if she were a thief.

When she went up to the study, Matilde did not know exactly what to look for. She moved a few books and picked up a piece of paper covered with her son's neat handwriting. She put on her glasses and saw it contained some notes on the probable testamentary interpretation of a letter a man left for his governess. She continued blindly, moving the pens that were scattered on the shelf without realizing it, her eyes darting around the room. Then she spied something that took her breath so completely away, she felt as if she might never breathe again.

A reading stand, which had been in the study downstairs until her husband's death, stood next to the table. It was a tall, narrow piece of furniture with two doors and a slanted piece of wood at the top. A large piece of white paper with a sketch of a human figure was pinned onto the slanted wood with a thumbtack. A nude woman with her legs spread, her sex unseemly exposed. A masculine hand held a long stick, as if it were searching inside.

Matilde flew out of the study, slamming the door violently behind her.

She tried hard not to think all day, but her son's behavior that evening forced her, for the first time, to make some connections that filled her with fear. Enea realized his mother had been in his rooms and reacted with uncontrollable fury. He had always behaved toward her with formal politeness, sometimes excessive, and had never raised his voice inside the walls of their home. That evening, he burst into the sitting room where Matilde was watching a movie on television, waving his arms like a madman and shouting at the top of his lungs.

"I hope you enjoyed yourself in my study. I hope you liked what you found. I noticed, you know, that you went to stick your nose in my things again!"

He raced out of the room in a fit. Then Matilde saw him come back a short while later, waving something around, which he hurled at the wall with all his might. The glass in a picture frame shattered, struck square in the middle by the two big iron keys that were hooked together on a brass ring. Matilde stared at that stranger, shaking for fear of physical danger.

She was struck by a horrible thought. She had read in the newspapers that after the last homicide the killer who was murdering couples had flown into a rage because the man behind the wheel had put the car into reverse and started it, attempting to escape the attack. After killing the young couple, the man had ripped the keys out of the ignition and hurled them far away in a triumphant affirmation of victory for getting the upper hand that time too. Or out of rage over the young man's rebellion. Reading the description in the newspaper, Matilde had pictured the image of a tall, stout, and somehow awkward man who was waving his arms around and flung the keys away. When Enea's tall, stout, awkward body stood out against the hall light, his face, hidden in the shadow of the dark sitting room, was caught obliquely by the flash of light from the television as he hurled the keys at the picture. The two images instantly became superimposed, finally merging completely into one.

That same night, after her son had gone out slamming the door, Matilde ended up torturing herself over the problem of the gun in spite of herself. The killer had used a twenty-two caliber for all of the murders, and Enea kept Nanni's gun somewhere in his study. Her husband had always carried it with him when he still worked the night shift at the hospital. When he died, Enea had wanted the gun as a keepsake. Matilde had no way of knowing for sure if it was a twenty-two or a thirty-two caliber, but there was a two in there somewhere. She was sure of it.

Whenever she felt tense, Matilde nibbled at the skin on the inside of her lips without even realizing it. Noticing the taste of blood, she finally decided to stop letting her imagination run wild. Maybe she was making a mountain out of a molehill. Goodness knows how many people owned that type of gun. At last she managed to boil down the problem that was worrying her to what she knew for sure. As far as the gun was concerned, the only thing that was certain was that Enea had inherited one. As for the machinery of suspicions put into motion by the disturbed case of scalpels, on thinking about it with a cool head, there was not even any reason to support it. At the last crime the killer had not even used a knife.

If all the uproar over the murders of the couples threatened to make even the most sensible people become carried away sooner or later, then she would be careful not to fall into the trap. She went to bed feeling more relieved.

3

Although he did not have any commitments that could really be defined as such, Enea Monterispoli spent his days bustling about. He would leave home every morning at exactly a quarter past eight, most often dressed in gray. He walked quickly down the path, opened the gate, and carefully closed it, and then started downhill, headed to the stop for the bus into the city. If the bus was a few minutes late he would start to pace impatiently back and forth on the sidewalk. After Enea's hours were reduced to a half-day, people in the neighborhood were even more convinced that his job in notary Colamele's office was only a favor the elderly professional did for Matilde. It gave her some freedom from her son's presence, and gave him an appearance of normality. The only one who did not think of it that way was Enea. If he did not arrive at work by nine o'clock in the morning when the notary's head secretary opened the office, he would have an anxiety attack.

Enea had never graduated from the university, even though he had passed the exams for his law degree with honors. Learning was second nature to him, and whatever he read, from the most scientific texts to the most obscure, he instantly committed to memory. There was no subject Enea could not discuss with complete command, even though he did not do so, because he was closemouthed. He did not have any biases against certain kinds of publications or rule anything out. When someone told him that he was nauseated by what was being produced in the field of knowledge and literature, and was going to take up reading the classics again, Enea reacted with disbelief. He knew the classics by heart and could quote from Sophocles to Apuleius, from Stendhal to Stadler as if he had them right in front of his eyes.

Everyone had their own theory about why he had not graduated. Matilde was convinced that the physical problems Enea had had as a child had influenced his brain's capabilities for logical progression. Otherwise it would not have been possible to explain why he had suddenly stopped working on his thesis on the systematic application of sentencing proceedings in order to devote himself to the study of Christian literatures of the East. In Andreino Colamele's opinion, Enea was simply an only child who had been spoiled by both his father and his mother. After coming into the inheritance from his father (though it was tied up by an airtight provision allowing Matilde to use it), he no longer believed he needed to commit himself to anything. So he freely indulged his intellectual caprices, which somewhat recalled his father, Nanni's, allowing him to roam from the art of the Pre-Raphaelites to the popular novel, and even comics.

Andreino Colamele was the only one who knew that Enea's presence in his notary office was anything but superfluous. Most of the time, Enea worked out complex corporate and inheritance problems without realizing he was doing such sophisticated, often innovative work. The research and final solutions came to him completely spontaneously. The fact that he had not even graduated from college put Colamele in the privileged position of appearing as if he were a benefactor.

Enea had gotten his light blue eyes and reddish brown hair from his mother, but the resemblance stopped there. Matilde was still a beautiful, tall woman with a calm face. Her hair had subtle white streaks and was styled carefully in small waves that curled around the nape of her neck. In contrast, Enea had a strikingly disharmonious body, having suffered from a light form of hypergonadism, complicated by a tendency toward hyperpituitarism. He was almost six feet two inches tall, and he had such long arms that when they hung at his sides they nearly reached the top of his knees. His weak chin seemed hardly able to support his jaw and mouth.

Enea always walked in a hurry, stepping heel first, then toes. His gait made his shoulders move up and down, as if they were driven by an internal piston. He covered a lot of miles every day, going from the bus stop to the notary Colamele's office and back again, not including the times he returned from the city on foot, whenever it was not raining or windy. But the exercise had no effect on his muscles. The passing years and the diabetes he had suffered from for some time had made him flabby. Enea was forty-eight years old, seventeen years younger than his mother, yet more and more often someone would mistake him for Matilde's husband. She would not have admitted it to anyone, but she would never have wanted a husband like her son.

"Good morning, Doctor," Colamele's head secretary would say when Enea came into the office. She called him Doctor, but treated him with an air of superiority, constantly repeating "come on, come on, hurry it up." He grumbled in reply.

As soon as he came inside the door, Enea closed himself up in the small room at the end of the hall, which had a desk and an old Remington typewriter, inherited from the original furniture in the office. The notary's offices were on the second floor of a building on via Arte della Lana. The windows in the large office where Andreino Colamele met with his clients looked out on the west side of the Orsanmichele church, with a beautiful view of the Linaioli and Rigattieri tabernacle and the marble San Marco by Donatello. The window in Enea's office, which was tall and narrow, made of lead-framed glass divided into lots of rectangles, faced an inner courtyard instead, in reality little more than an air vent.

When he started his work in the morning, Enea would find Andreino Colamele's notes already lying on the roller of the old Remington with the list of work for the day. He stayed bent over the papers without lifting his head until he heard the church bells chime twelve o'clock. Then he gathered the papers he had prepared, complete with a handwritten memo in which he explained the methods he had followed and the specific precedents he had referred to. He went to hand them over to Colamele if the notary was free. Otherwise, he gave them to the head secretary, who took them with a slight nod of assent, placing them in the box of files to be examined.

Enea had decided to reduce his work hours to a half-day when he met Nanda. At first his mother was extremely worried about what she viewed as a rash decision, already imagining what people would say and picturing what it would be like with her son around the house all afternoon becoming more and more lifeless and awkward. But then she had adapted to the new situation, because, if anything, Enea went out more than before.

❧

After the visit from the police, Matilde Monterispoli was gripped by a constant state of anxiety. She could not go to the window without being afraid of seeing the two men planted in front of her door or hear the doorbell ring without feeling her stomach knot up. The two policemen's brief stay within the walls of her home had left her with a sense of estrangement, especially with regard to her sitting room, where they had been. She no longer spent any time there, not even a few minutes.

Since she was a practical woman, she realized that if she let her emotions devour her, she would make herself sick. So she devoted her time to doing things to keep herself busy. She started to take care of the household purchases personally and to clean the closets, which were already in perfect order. Before long, she told herself she had to find something else to do, something that would at least get her out with other people. One evening when she was feeling particularly depressed, she decided to pay a visit to an elderly lady, over ninety years old, who lived alone in an apartment at the top of viale Volta. It was just a few bus stops away, and she had not seen her for months.

Right after dinner she called to let the woman know she was coming to visit, and prepared a small tray of cookies. She calculated that the trip there and back, and the time to chat a while, would take her an hour, more or less. Instead, more than two hours passed by. The sweet old lady, a tiny, wise woman dressed in black and white silk, had only one ailment that came from age—she suffered from insomnia and spent the night speculating about her fellow human beings. She kept Matilde there talking nonstop about how much the neighborhood had changed since she had moved there, how she did not much like the changes, and how everyone's lives had become worse.

"But I don't want to die," she said at a certain point, "because so much can still happen." She leaned forward, slapping her bony hand on Matilde's knee. "You heard, didn't you? They're about to arrest Racconigi!"

Racconigi was a building contractor who had become outrageously rich in the space of a few years. The old families of the city, as if by tacit agreement, disdainfully excluded him from their circles.

"It's about time," answered Matilde. "If they don't stop him, he'll end up ruining what little good we have left. They even say he intends to submit a project to turn the Palazzo Vecchio into a hotel."

The old lady shook her head. "Palazzo Vecchio! Of course not! They're arresting him because he's the Monster." She launched into a complex explanation demonstrating why Racconigi was the Monster. "You remember, don't you, the first time a young woman's corpse was mutilated? It must have been the second or third murder. A friend of mine who is a psychiatrist— I can't tell you his name—maintains that up until that moment the killer hadn't taken his rage out on the corpses because his latent sadistic sexual instincts hadn't emerged yet. Just think, I didn't even know what that word meant. He had to explain it to me. At any rate, he said that a Black Mass was what made them manifest. That was exactly when Racconigi started to organize just that, Black Masses, at his villa in Mugello."

~~~~~~~~~~

Matilde replied she had never heard that Black Masses should be added to Racconigi's numerous diabolical dealings. She added, "I've heard about the theory of the manifestation of sadistic sexual impulses too. It was in connection with a certain kind of film. I don't remember in which newspaper, but I read that on the days of the various homicides, some theaters in the city were showing one of those horrible movies. The ones so full of killing and bloodshed that I don't know how they can be allowed."

"Horrible movies or Black Masses, what difference does it make?" the old lady said, convinced that every line of reasoning, even if contradictory, should be adopted if it could be used to support her point. "Racconigi certainly doesn't lack the means to go to the movies."

Matilde had been keeping her eye on the time for a while so she could avoid standing on the street to wait for the bus to San Domenico, which came by less often at that hour. She broke off the conversation abruptly and said goodbye, promising to come back again soon.

When she left, she just had to cross the road to reach the bus stop. A little ways down the street there was one of those movie theaters she and the elderly woman had talked about. It had a terrible reputation in the neighborhood. So bad that the residents (with Matilde at the lead) had presented a petition to have it shut down. The movie must have ended just then, because a few people were trickling out, with their heads down to hide their faces. They were all men, and each one went off in a different direction.

Looking toward the entrance of the theater, less out of curiosity than for fear she would be mistaken for one of the moviegoers, Matilde's eyes caught sight of a tall, awkward man. His arms were disproportionately long, his oval head sunk into his shoulders, and he stood out like a large shadow against the lights of the theater entrance. She squinted so she could see the person better. There seemed to be no doubt. The man was Enea. She burned with shame at seeing her son come out of a place like that, and she quickly turned away so he would not recognize her.

She stayed up late that night. As the hours passed by, she formed an image of Enea that was like none she had ever had before. A big, cumbersome stranger who roamed around her house, with his own life and his own secrets that made her afraid. The fact that she had given birth to him seemed remote and inessential. Enea came home very late and paced back and forth in his study all night. From his heavy footsteps and hasty comings and goings, Matilde knew intuitively that he must not even have stopped to take his shoes off and put on his slippers. He probably had not taken his coat off either. He was extremely upset.

As Matilde walked down the avenue the next day, she passed in front of the movie posters at the theater. They were red and showed a man with a distorted face holding a long dagger in his hand, stabbing a terrorized woman who vainly tried to protect herself.

4

Nanda was a young woman a little over twenty years old who lived by her wits, and like some newborn babies, she mistook day for night. She would get up at one in the afternoon and start to roam the streets. First she searched for her prey to rob, and then for her pusher, who had to sell her more heroin.

Enea met her on the number 7 bus one evening. They had both gotten on at Piazza San Marco. He was headed for home, and she had decided to get off right after she lifted the wallet off of that great big, tall, dull-looking man. But when Nanda got close to him, pretending to stumble, and slipped her hand in his pocket, Enea caught her by the wrist. He turned around with a look of both surprise and pain as his eyes fell on the thin, blond woman in a clinging, little yellow knit dress, who was trying to rob him.

"What are you doing?" he asked her. "Why don't you ask first, instead of just taking it?"

Enea came home very late that night, and during the hours spent with Nanda he made a pledge to himself that would last a long time.

Nanda lived in an attic room on via Panicale. She had been doing drugs for three years. Her husband insisted he never wanted to see her again, but went looking for her now and then, promising her that if she would get some treatment he would take her back. Flanked on both sides by walls of peeling plaster, a steep, narrow staircase ran up to Nanda's room. There was no running water or even a bathroom inside. The bathroom was just beyond a small door in the attic. For Nanda, the room was just a place to sleep on the few nights she remembered to go there. She would never have given it a thought if Enea had not insisted that she could not continue to live like that.

He was so obstinate about it that he made her move into a studio apartment on via de' Renai, just off the Arno River. He was the one who found the apartment for her, and he would pay for it. It was not a luxury apartment, but it was furnished in a dignified manner, with a double bed, an easy chair, a table, and an armoire. There were even some prints hanging on the walls and curtains in the windows, and the red tile floor was protected by a coir rug. The rent was extremely high because apartments like those were destined for rich men who used them as *pied-à-terre,* places to take their lovers. In fact, they were all *à-terre,* with the apartment doors located directly on the street or immediately inside the building's main entrance.

The new living arrangement did not make Nanda's habits any more regular. After a period of relative tranquility, she started to hit the streets again at night, caught up in her hectic search for money and pushers. At first, Enea vaguely hoped he could somehow save the young woman. Then, little by little he perfected a theory that, in his opinion, was flawless. Precisely because it was flawless, it could not fail to produce results.

Nanda had told him about how her childhood had been devastated by her family's poverty, economic and moral. Love had been crushed by hardships, with a passive mother and a violent father who had thrown his own daughter on the bed one day and raped her. She had endured the situation in silence to avoid hurting her mother. As soon as she could, she ran away from home. Since then, she had never seen her parents again. She had always been evasive about her marriage to Aldo Mazzacane, a county employee, as if it were simply a matter of some kind of sad casualty of loneliness.

Not much time went by before Enea discovered the truth. He arrived at the apartment on via de' Renai one day and found Aldo Mazzacane there. The dark-haired young man had a serious face and was yelling at Nanda in a voice torn with desperation. Nanda threw everything within her reach at Aldo, and when Enea tried to calm her down she threw a plate strewn with leftover salad at him too, shouting at him to mind his own business. Then she ran out.

That was how Enea came to find out the true story of Nanda's life from her ex-husband, who continued to call her "my wife" despite their divorce and long separation. In reality, her parents were two good people. Her father worked as a goldsmith and her mother was a bank clerk. When Aldo Mazzacane asked Nanda to marry him, she was already addicted to heroin, but he did not know yet. Since the day of their wedding, she had gotten him into every kind of trouble imaginable, spending everything he earned, selling things from their home, and stealing from their friends. She was stopped by the police two times. Only the intervention of an acquaintance saved her from the worst. In the end, there was a robbery at her father's shop, and everyone was convinced the inside tip had come from Nanda.

"Even so," added Mazzacane, his voice faint from humiliation, "my wife has a big heart. She was led astray by the bad company she kept. If only she could manage to break away from that awful circle of people! I'm sure she would go back to being the nice girl her parents talk about. If it were just up to me, I'd drop her for good. I'd resign myself to it. But her mother, that poor woman. When she's so desperate she can't take it any more, she comes looking for me, and begs me to bring her some news. What does she expect? Most of the time I lie. But I can't shirk my obligation to see how her daughter is doing now and then."

They had been seeing each other for three months when Enea got the idea to take Nanda a box of chocolates. The young woman had been eating only sweet things for a while. When he arrived, her hair was nicely combed and she was wearing a skirt with red poppies on it and a white blouse instead of the usual jeans and sweater. She accepted the chocolates as if they were some incredible gift. Suddenly, she tossed the box on the table and laughingly pushed Enea to make him fall on the bed. She moved toward Enea, blocking his legs with hers, and started to unbutton her blouse, revealing her breasts, which were almost nonexistent, with large dark nipples and areolas that spread out like rays.

Enea jerked back, blushing. "No, come on now. No! What are you doing? You don't understand . . . cover yourself up."

Nanda did not cover herself up. She stood still in front of him, with her hands on her hips. "Well then, could you tell me what you want from me? No, I really don't understand you."

"I only want to help you," mumbled Enea. "This is the first time I've encountered pain. The spectacle of pain is unbearable."

She did not give up. She quickly slipped off her skirt, and was not wearing anything underneath it. She sat down on his knees and clasped her skinny arms around his neck, rubbing his forehead with her chin and moving herself against him without stopping at all. At first, Enea grabbed her by the hips to make her get up. Yet when he felt her smooth skin under his fingers he was so surprised, unable to believe that a person's body could be so soft. Nanda moaned, taking his hand to put it on her breast. All of a sudden, Enea completely lost his senses. He became frenzied, feeling, touching, searching, unable to control himself. When Nanda opened her legs, guiding his fingers inside her, Enea saw such an ecstatic expression on her face that he was moved to tears. He moved his large hand, following the rhythm that Nanda set, while her body arched and writhed, relaxed, and then became taut again. At last he saw she was exhausted, laying back against him as if she were lifeless.

But she was not lifeless. She sprang up, laughing, and started to unbutton his pants. "Now it's your turn," she whispered. Enea did not grab her wrist in time. She was already touching him, and stopped at once, dumbfounded by what she discovered. "Didn't you like it?" she asked. She noticed Enea's expression and drew back her hand. "You shouldn't worry about it. It happens to a lot of guys," she said, but her voice lacked conviction.

She put her clothes back on, took a couple of steps around the room, and moved up to him again. "If it's fine for you that way, it's fine for me too. You liked it at least a little, didn't you?"

Enea nodded yes, shaking his head up and down.

5

Matilde followed her son's nocturnal movements through the sounds that echoed back to her ears. She caught his footsteps crossing the wood floor above her bedroom, the study door creaking open several times during the night, feet shuffling down the stone stairs and across the runner in the hallway to the kitchen, and finally the refrigerator door closing. Since he had developed diabetes, Enea constantly made hurried trips to the bathroom. He was tormented by an unquenchable thirst that the bottle of mineral water he took up to the study every night could not satisfy. It drove him out of his refuge around two o'clock, carrying him off to the kitchen to get some more to drink.

She imagined her son sitting at the big wooden table reading or taking notes, or in the workshop next to it, absorbed in making one of his carvings. When they were finished, he put them on a pile in a big open box in a corner of the room, and never touched them again. Hunched over, his oval shaped head bowed over the work at hand, his big body wrapped in the beige velvet bathrobe he used both in the cold of winter and the heat of summer, wearing his old brown leather slippers.

Matilde knew about the bathrobe and slippers because she had seen them in Enea's rooms, not because her son had ever worn those clothes in front of her. When he came out of his room in the morning, he was already fully dressed, ready to go out. He had his own private bath, located directly off his bedroom, and when he came downstairs to go to bed at night, Matilde never happened to see him. She only heard him coming from the end of the hall.

It was through those sounds that Matilde reconstructed Enea's movements on the nights of the murders too. For several years her son had been going out every evening on the weekend, and coming home in the middle of the night. Just recently he had changed his routine, going out on workdays too, without worrying about whether he had to get up early the next morning.

Matilde could not go to sleep until he was back home. In those long hours of waiting, spent with her ears straining to catch the crunch of the gravel under Enea's footsteps as he returned home, she had learned not to think about anything. Lately though, her thoughts took shape and unraveled irresistibly, with no clear contours yet connected by a single thread of logic. If she had forced herself to put the meaning of those nocturnal meditations into words, she would have had to admit she had broken the resolution she had made to herself to keep her imagination bridled within the limits of what was certain. More and more often she happened to compare every memory, every one of her son's actions, past and present, with the suspicion that had cropped into her head. She tried as hard as she could to get her mind back on something concrete. When she succeeded, she regretted having a feeble mind that yielded to the suggestion of sleepless nights. Yet most of the time, she remained trapped by her fears.

She had read that the killer always struck before holidays when there was a new moon and the sky was darker. The first murder was committed many years earlier, and Enea was not even thirty yet. That was when Enea had begun working in Colamele's office and going out on weekends. Matilde was almost happy about it. She had always been afraid her son would feel bad about his appearance and withdraw into a shell for the rest of his life. That he was going out made her think he had found interests beyond the four walls of their home and, in particular, his rooms. Nevertheless, she could not resist warning him about the outside world.

"Be careful who you talk to," she would say. "Always ask yourself why someone comes up to you, and what they want from you."

Enea would shake his big head, telling her not to worry. He knew more about life than she did.

A man, the husband of one of the two victims, had been arrested for the first homicide and convicted of the murder. There had been no more talk about it until six years later, when another couple had been slaughtered, again in a car, and again on the outskirts of the city. With the prisoner inconveniently behind bars, the investigators had taken some time before admitting he could not have been the one who killed the second couple. It had taken an officer with a long memory to recall a bullet kept in the file from the first homicide. He had gone to retrieve it, and asked for a ballistics test, which showed beyond any doubt that the weapon and the type of bullets used in the two homicides were the same.

Lying in bed with her eyes open in the dark, Matilde remembered what the newspapers had written then. At the second homicide the young woman had been lifted out of the car and her body cut by dozens of "puncture and slash wounds" (the words from the report published in the press were still embedded in her memory). The murderer had torn her pants and underwear with a knife to remove them, as though he had felt an irrepressible revulsion toward touching the pieces of clothing.

A memory came effortlessly to Matilde's mind, of a day many years before. The garden had been rocked by a violent storm that had made all the windows in the house rattle. There were clothes hanging out to dry in the back, and the housekeeper was out somewhere. Matilde was in her bathrobe, her hair still wet from the shower, and had asked Enea to run out quickly and bring the wash in before the wind ripped everything off the clotheslines. Her son had run outside, taken the clothes down, and come back inside with his arms full as he passed by the kitchen door. She had begun folding their things on the marble table. Enea set about helping her, with that eager look he got on his face when he could make himself useful. He happened to pick up a bra. He instantly jerked back as if he had been bitten by a snake, and let it fall.

The move to via de' Renai had not proved to be the answer to all of Nanda's problems. Enea told her one day that he could not stand to see her suffering the way she was. She started to yell. "Suffering? But what suffering are you talking about? I feel just fine like this. Get me some dope and you'll see how fine I feel. Do you understand? Do you? Get me the dope, if you don't want to see me suffering!"

~~~~~~~~~~~~~~~~~~~~

So Enea started to pass substantial amounts of money along to her, until he realized he was on the verge of draining everything out of his bank account. Nanda seemed more peaceful those days, and when Enea would visit her she made him coffee and told him how she spent her days. She even washed her hair, which became a shinier, lighter blond. If it had not been for the dark circles under her eyes and her sunken cheeks, she would almost be pretty.

After that first time on the bed she had not undressed in front of him again. Every time they met he would shake from fear she would do it again. At the same time, he was dying with the desire to see her do it another time. Then one night she unexpectedly sat with his arms around her, beginning to moan and writhe again. Since then, when he arrived at via de' Renai Enea always hoped that Nanda would come up close to him. He would never risk making the first move. The young woman had to be the one to decide how and when, because that was the only way he could be sure she would like to do it too.

If he had had to explain what kind of emotion tied him to Nanda, Enea would not have hesitated to call it love. Their unconsummated relations seemed much more than he had ever imagined he could have in those long hours of loneliness. Never having experienced anything like it or even something of a different kind, for him that was the only way to love someone.

He was happy about how things were going, except when Nanda's head drooped (which happened when she closed herself in the bathroom and came out a little later, buttoning the sleeve of her blouse), or when she burst into anger for no apparent reason. In any case, it was better than knowing she was out wandering the streets to look for money for drugs. This was why Enea became more and more generous with the amounts of money he gave her. Then one day at Colamele's office, he received a phone call from the manager of his bank. This was the first time the bank had ever tried to get in touch with him. He was totally stunned until the voice belonging to the name of the person the secretary had announced reached his ears.

"I don't want to seem indiscreet," the man said cautiously. "Though I'm calling, it's not in a professional capacity. It's out of the friendship I have with your mother and felt for your father too." It seemed to Enea as if he already knew each word the man was going to say. "It has been brought to my attention that recently your withdrawals have grown increasingly frequent and increasingly large."

Enea replied that to his knowledge he had not overdrawn his account, and the manager caught the tension in his voice. "But no, of course not," he hastened to say. "It's not a matter of insufficient funds. That's the last thing we'd need! But even if it were the case, can you imagine we would have any problem with a person like yourself?" From that moment on, he began using the impersonal "we" as he spoke. They were just worried he might be having some difficulties, but they were at his service for whatever kind of advice he might need.

After the conversation with the manager, Enea had to let Nanda know that for a while he would have to scrimp on the money he gave her. He did not go into details about the telephone call or about being afraid that the bank might inform his mother, but the young woman seemed to understand that the problems had to be serious.

"Don't worry. You mustn't worry," she reassured him, without asking any questions. "I'll make do somehow. For now, if nothing else, I've had time to catch my breath again." From then on, she started to disappear for long stretches of time again, which tore Enea up inside and kept him lying awake in misery for entire nights.

It was in those days that Enea met George Lockridge, whom he had not seen for many years. He was a landscape painter from England who used to spend time with Enea's family when his father was still alive. George lived in a farmhouse outside the city now. Since his style of painting was not in demand anymore, he claimed he made a living as an art restorer and dealer. As a young man, he had been perennially plagued by anxiety, which made his face break out in red blotches that stood out against his light complexion, and by nervous tics that made his body twitch. Old age seemed to have granted him the dignity possessed by those who watch life with a certain detachment.

George had recognized Enea first, running into him on via de' Calzaiuoli. He blocked his way, taking hold of his arm, and Enea struggled to jog his memory for the name of his father's friend. Then he remembered the kind English painter who used to live in a large attic apartment, just beyond their house. People said he was homosexual and preyed upon the young schoolboys that the mothers in the city entrusted to his artistic sensibility so he would polish their rough edges.

"Well look who's here! It's dear Enea," he said, shaking his hand with his slender, ice-cold fingers. "You look just the same as you did thirty years ago." He glanced at him sideways through his thick glasses and cracked a slight smile. "Or at least, just the same for a trained eye like mine."

Enea's eyes met his, feeling slightly ill at ease as he saw what a state he was reduced to. He was skinny as a rail and dressed in a multicolored, striped knit top, flannel trousers, and heavy leather sandals worn with red woolen socks.

"I'm happy to see you," he said. Not wanting to lie about his reaction, he added, "I'm just a little taken aback by your white hair."

He was touched though, by the encounter.

The fortuitous occasion of seeing the Englishman again gave Enea the opportunity to continue helping Nanda.

6

"Have you heard?" Matilde said to her son, while she served herself some soup from the tureen. "They've formed an anti-Monster squad."

"I've heard, I've heard," Enea replied, sitting down at the table and unfolding his napkin to put it on his lap. He had just come from his bedroom at the end of the hall. As he did every evening before dinner, he had gone into his room, closing the door behind him, to give himself his shot of insulin, and he was in a hurry to eat.

Matilde was bent on finding a way to keep the conversation going. She knew she had to proceed very cautiously if she did not want her son to clam up in one of his long silences. She could not think of anything to say, though, other than that the thought of those tortured bodies was unbearable. "He must use an extremely sharp knife," she murmured. A little later she added, "Or a scalpel."

Enea sat still with his hand in midair, continuing to stare at the plate and waiting for his mother to finally pass him the tureen of soup. "Mama, you know that after I take the insulin I have to eat something."

Matilde pushed the soup toward him. After swallowing a few spoonfuls, more out of habit than because she was hungry, she went on, "They're saying that the city is under siege at night. They're stopping almost anybody, but mainly men who are out alone. Maybe it would be better if you didn't go out for now." She glanced up to see her son's reaction, but it seemed as if he had not heard her. "I worry when you're out," she began again, in a complaining voice she could hardly recognize.

"But you shouldn't worry," Enea finally made up his mind to answer. "That's what is really monstrous. Terrorizing people."

"Be careful, Enea," Matilde said. "Be careful."

He lifted his head up to look at her. "Mama, you're getting old. Careful about what?"

"Nothing," Matilde broke off, unable to continue. "You know, a letter came for you. It arrived from Edinburgh. It's from some man named Morris. Professor Robert Morris, from an institute of parapsychology." She wiped her mouth with the napkin, dabbing persistently at the corners. "Who knows how he managed to get your address."

Enea said he had sent it to him himself, because Morris was conducting some interesting experiments with fish. "He puts three fish in an aquarium. It seems that the one slated to be taken out of the water warns the other fish about the impending danger and acts differently from the other two. It thrashes about as if it were crazy and swims in circles as though trying to escape its destiny."

"Do you really believe these things?" asked Matilde.

"I'm not that thoroughly familiar with these experiments. I'd like to know more about them. If it's true—as it is—that the human mind doesn't utilize all of the capabilities locked inside, then the possibility of para-psychological communication can't be ruled out."

"Maybe," said Matilde. "Then who knows what they'll ask you for in return."

When her son asked her in return for what, Matilde did not know what to answer, except that perhaps they would demand some kind of fee or subscription, or even make him participate in séances. Enea laughed, shaking his head. Then he became totally absorbed in a long speech about how the human mind forced patently irreconcilable points of departure and arrival into the usual, narrow limits it imposed itself. He concluded, saying that if Arthur Koestler had decided to leave his estate to the University of Edinburgh so that they would create an endowed chair in parapsychology, then at least the subject warranted further investigation.

"Maybe," repeated Matilde. "But in the end, you can at least tell me how much money they want you to pay."

"You should quit being so suspicious. It wears people out if they look for dark meanings in everything that seems out of the ordinary."

"I know that being suspicious has often saved me from the worst," replied Matilde, piqued.

Enea would never have thought about life in terms of destiny. Yet while he hurriedly went down the dark streets behind Piazza della Signoria and his mother sat watching a television exposé on the multiple murders, a kind of destiny was unfolding for him as it was for her.

Enea was looking for George Lockridge. He was supposed to meet him in some dingy hole on via Vacchereccia, which the Englishman called "my shop."

Since their first meeting, Enea and Lockridge had seen each other a couple more times. The first time was at George's insistence. Then they met by chance (or at least Enea thought so), on via de' Calzaiuoli again, which Enea went down twice a day to go to Colamele's office and to return home again.

It had not taken George Lockridge long to guess that Enea had some trouble or difficulties, immediately recognizable as a "cash shortfall." He did not stop to ask himself why he might need it. He was already too loaded with his own troubles to be able to worry about anyone else's. Furthermore, since he was convinced that only those who did not submit to the despicable rules of normality were truly free, he thought economic problems were little more than a temporary indisposition that could be solved case by case with improvised interventions.

When they had met the first time, the Englishman had asked Enea what he did during the day and how his mother, one of the most beautiful women he had ever met, was doing. Upon finding out they rarely went to their country house at Impruneta, and that Nanni's collection of paintings was still hanging in the large room on the first floor, he started to become agitated.

"Paintings are like human beings," he said. "They feel loneliness and are afraid of the dark. Would you shut a beautiful woman up in a humid room with all the windows closed? No, of course you wouldn't shut her up inside, because she would wither, with no remedy. It's the same thing with paintings."

"There's no problem," Enea smiled. "The estate manager's wife opens all of the windows regularly to air out the house. Mama and I also go out there at least a couple of times a year to make sure everything is in order."

But the Englishman turned a deaf ear. "I can't imagine those beautiful landscapes by Palizzi or those splendid portraits by Piccio abandoned in a house that's all closed up in the middle of some hills. It would be better if you gave them to a museum. No one has the right to lock beauty away."

He added that, among other things, they were worth a fortune. These days, how could someone neglect a fortune of such value, not only artistic but also economic, that way? Have any of the paintings from the collection ever been sold by any chance?

"Don't worry about it," Enea reassured him, "all of the paintings are still there, each one hanging in its place."

"And those two little jewels, those French fipple flutes?" the Englishman persisted. "If I'm not mistaken, they were from the seventeenth century. Your father kept them on the veranda, in the small King George III credenza, running the risk they would be ruined."

"Those are still there too," Enea answered.

George Lockridge recalled each of the valuable pieces of the Monterispoli estate one by one, including the beautiful Davenport place settings in stone china and the delicate silverware by Georg Jensen. "To think," he said, "that one of those rare pieces alone would be enough to solve the problems of not just one family, but ten." He looked up at Enea, squeezing his arm. "Certainly you're not in need of money, but if by any chance you were . . ."

Enea let it slip that everyone, for one reason or another, could use more money. Lockridge replied that all it would take was to go and get one of the paintings in the collection and something could be arranged.

"I remember a little Rosai, a road running between some tall houses, with two men in the middle of it, who seem to dominate the landscape. I'd be curious to see how well it's been preserved. You know, I was the one who convinced your father to buy it when some fellow from Compiobbi died. The heirs didn't realize what a fortune they had right in their own hands."

At first, Lockridge thought about having the Rosai left with him, with the excuse that he wanted to enjoy it for a while. He could take some time to search for a buyer, and then substitute a copy in its place. But a scheme like that could only work once he told himself, assuming that Enea fell for it. Enea had grown up surrounded by those paintings, and certainly he could tell the difference between the real ones and the fakes, no matter how skillfully the copy might be executed. It would be much better to play on his need for money and make him understand that the collection could be an inexhaustible source of prosperity for the both of them.

That was how it went. Enea was running to cash in on the proceeds from the sale and pick up the copy. Then he would take it to the Impruneta house the next day and hang it on the wall between *The Carts* by Fattori and *The Arno* by De Tivoli, where the authentic Rosai had been until a short while before.

When he went into the dingy hole, he found the Englishman standing with the copy of the Rosai rolled up in an old newspaper in one hand, and a wad of bills in the other.

"Take it, take it," said Lockridge. "Don't bother thanking me. I did it just because. Don't ask me to do it again. Be careful. The paint should be dry by now, but don't hold it too tight."

The Englishman gave Enea a substantial amount of money, even though it represented less than one-twentieth of the painting's actual value. Lockridge had tried to figure out just the right split. He could not give Enea too little, because of the risk that he would become discouraged and not do it again. He could not give him too much either if he did not want him to develop a taste for high prices. In the end, he had decided to give him exactly one-fourth of the entire sum. After all, he needed to compensate himself for the work he put into making the copy, which he had painted with the utmost care, working nights too.

After picking up the money, Enea was sure he would not see George Lockridge again. That amount would be enough for him to pay three months rent for the apartment and enable Nanda to go on for a while. Then he would see. He still had not given up hope that the young woman would make up her mind to get some treatment.

When he arrived at via de' Renai, out of breath and red in the face from the strain of running, Nanda was not at home. He looked for her in all of the alleys and all of the squares where he thought he might be able to find her, going as far as Borgo Pinti and then up to Piazzale Donatello, and at last heading back toward Porta della Croce. He took long strides as he walked, his arms dangling at his sides, his oval shaped head thrown forward, his eyes piercing the dark entryways and scrutinizing the shapes of the bodies that were crouched along the sidewalk.

He caught sight of Nanda when it was almost daybreak. She was squatting against a wall under the colonnade of the Loggia del Grano. Her eyes were closed and she had a strip of rubber stretched around her arm, biting into her pale skin. There was a thin man with an excited face, wearing a light, full-length overcoat standing beside her. He was kicking every inch of her body and knocking her around, hitting her head against the wall. He yelled at her to stop pretending she didn't hear him, because he wasn't leaving if she didn't cough up the cash. He might have been an idiot to give her the dope without making her pay up front, but he wasn't so dumb that he'd let her off the hook without at least splitting her head open like a watermelon.

Enea reacted without realizing what he was doing. He hit the man on the shoulders. Then he grabbed him by the scruff of the neck and lifted him off the ground and started to shake him, making him bounce in the air like an empty sack. The more he shook him, the more his anger welled. The man's head was jerking back and forth, his neck about to snap. As if sensing that something really serious might happen, Nanda opened her eyes and started to groan.

"Enea, help me," she said. "Help me! Take me home!"

If she had begged him to calm down and not hurt the pusher, he would not have stopped, but that meek appeal caught him by surprise. Enea dropped the man, who fell to the ground as if in pieces. He bent over Nanda and lifted her up, holding her body with her arm against him and her hand tucked under his armpit so that he could support her better. He carried her like that all the way to via de' Renai.

When they were inside, he laid her down on the bed, took off the strip of rubber, and rolled down her sleeve. He covered her with the blanket. That was when he saw the syringe caught in her knit top. He took it out delicately so he would not ruin the material, and then held it up in front of his eyes, recognizing something familiar about it. It was an insulin syringe, like the kind he used. A strong rush of emotion made his throat tighten.

7

For many years Matilde had lived with the thought of death as her constant companion. She could not have said when it started. One day she just stopped making plans, telling herself that she would not have had the time to finish them anyway, or at least to enjoy working on them.

The first time she had thought of herself as old was when she had read in the newspaper about a woman, just a few years younger than she, who had died in a car accident, and was referred to as "the elderly lady." Then she looked at her own image with detachment and suddenly concluded that her time had passed.

When people her age had started to die, she had not been that surprised. She knew she was in the high-risk category, as Nanni would say when speaking about patients of his who were getting on in years. Yet the idea of a violent death, striking from afar on top of it, deeply upset her. She had always seen herself passing away in her bed, with a priest by her side helping her to cross over life's threshold. If she thought about her son, Enea, she imagined him standing a few steps behind the priest, his face in the shadows. He was sorrowful yet aware that the time always comes for mothers to die and for their children to cry over them, at least for that brief period of mourning imposed for the sake of propriety.

When she had discovered the scalpels out of place, all at once she had felt how very real the possibility was that death might be something different from a woman passing away in her own bed with the comfort of a prayer. Death could also treacherously strike down young lives amid great bloodshed, and then be exposed on the pages of newspapers, without a shred of modesty.

With that image weighing on her mind, she walked up to the fireplace, staring at the case of scalpels. She tapped it with her forefinger, budging it a couple of inches to the left, then pushed it back to the right until the tip of the buckle was perfectly perpendicular to the black spot in the marble. She picked up the case, turned around, moved away a few steps, walked back, and put it on the mantel again. The buckle fell to the left of the spot, just as it was when she had found it out of place. She imagined her son making the very same movements.

As a boy, Enea immensely loved using all kinds of knives. He was surprisingly skillful when he set about cutting or carving. If a roast or chicken was served at the dinner table, he was always the one to prepare the servings, delicately carving the meat into even, thin slices. He cut the chickens into pieces as if he knew everything about their anatomy and could follow the contours exactly as nature had made them. Nanni was thoroughly delighted with the aptitude his son had, and even showed it off when someone came over for dinner. He used to say all the time that Enea had already found his profession. Sooner or later he would take him along in the operating room to have him help out cutting those chickens he had for patients.

One day Enea had looked at him, his eyes intent and face flushed by emotion, and said he would like to have a try at it. Nanni had burst out laughing. It was settled that he would grow up and become a surgeon. He would keep a position at the hospital all ready for Enea.

The killer who was murdering couples possessed the same skill that Enea had with sharp instruments. He might work in a tannery, the newspapers said, or be a carver, or maybe even a doctor, given the professional manner in which he had removed entire areas of the breast or pubis from the women's dead bodies, exhibiting speed and precision. He had another skill in common with Enea. When he fired a gun, he hit the mark on the first shot.

Matilde moved away from the fireplace, forcing herself not to give in to those morbid fantasies. She put on her coat and left the house, thinking that a short walk would clear her head and lift the pall of death she sensed upon her.

She set out toward Piazza San Domenico, thinking she would go as far as the Camerata Hospital. She soon realized it would be impossible for her not to think about the killer. The city could not forget about it, and in fact, as the days passed by it seemed all the more wrapped up in the story. A group of people had gathered in front of the newspaper stand, engaged in loud discussion and exchanging jokes veiled in biting irony about the Monster. Matilde thought it was shameful that anyone could try to joke about something so horrible. She did not notice the uneasiness, and perhaps fear, behind their blustering, sharp laughter.

She lengthened her stride, nodding brusquely in reply to the newspaper vendor's greeting. She walked straight down the street until she came upon Mariano Pizzoccheri standing in front of her. He had planted himself in the middle of the sidewalk and was staring at her, waiting for her eyes to meet his. Matilde smiled faintly, and moved to the side so she could continue on, but he spread his arms wide open to block her way.

"We live just a few steps away from one another," he said, "but we never see each other. It took the Monster to get you to come out of your house, eh?"

Matilde replied that she went out regularly for her walks and, if anything, he was the one who had become lazy.

Mariano Pizzoccheri had always worked as an insurance agent, until he had decided to give up the business and leave it to his son. Since he had retired, he spent his days sitting in an armchair with pencil in hand to write short poems and stories on large pieces of white paper that still had not found someone who might appreciate them. He tried to read them to anyone he met. Sometimes he managed to do so with Matilde, forcing her to listen to them after he had surprised her sitting on the low wall under the horse chestnut trees of the Badia Fiesolana church grounds. He even went to such lengths as visiting her in her home.

That morning he did not have any poems to read. Besides being a poet and writer, Pizzoccheri was convinced he was a sharp-minded thinker. Lately he had applied this gift to elaborating a theory about the killer who was murdering couples. He went up to Matilde, took her arm so he could adjust his pace to hers, and started to expound his theory.

"They can't tell me that finding him is so difficult after all," he said. "A far cry from a needle in a haystack.

51

If they knew how to use their heads, they would close in on a suspect, I assure you."

Pizzoccheri loved the kind of language used in the newspapers, and often without even realizing it, he made it his own. As a result, if he had to talk about a blitz or a manhunt or even an alarm, he inevitably paired them up with the verb "to spring." He could not find anything better than "close in" for a circle or a net, or even for a suspect, who was regularly closed in upon to make him take responsibility.

"Just for starters," he continued, "the man lives alone. There's no doubt about that at all. Even the police have realized it."

"Alone?" asked Matilde, making him stand still for a moment. "Alone, you say?"

"Precisely." Pizzoccheri was very satisfied with the result. He could hardly believe he had actually captured Matilde Monterispoli's attention. He continued quickly so he would not lose the advantage. "Who do you imagine he would live with, a man like that? Nothing, except a profound estrangement . . . *estrange-ment* . . . from the rest of the world can lead a human being to that state. Are you convinced?" Taking her silence for agreement, he tightened his hold on her arm and obliged her to adjust her pace to his, which had become measured, as if they were in a march.

They had reached the Camerata Hospital and set out along via della Piazzola. The street sloped down, bound by the tall, moss-covered walls of the villa parks. The branches of the oak trees were so laden with leaves that they blocked the sun. Matilde shivered, sorry she had continued in that direction. The air had turned cold and the smell of damp soil stung her nose.

"Now then," Pizzoccheri was saying, "how many men who live alone do you imagine there might be in this city? A thousand? Two thousand?" Meanwhile, he walked, tromping one foot after the other, and Matilde trudged along beside him, her face absorbed, eyes wide with apprehension.

"But if he really lives alone," she said, "then it's likely they'll catch him."

"It's a matter of days before the circle will close in. I told you. I already sent a letter with my observations both to the police and to the magistrate's office. But my investigation doesn't end here. No, it certainly does not end here. That man shoots like a professional, as if he were born with a gun in his hand. In fact . . ." He stopped all of a sudden and looked Matilde straight in the eye with a serious expression, in order to convey the importance of the revelation that he was about to make. "I wouldn't be surprised if he were a policeman," he whispered. "For that matter, it is the same caliber, you know? The caliber is the same as the regulation issue." He vigorously nodded in affirmation and started to walk again, dragging her along behind him. "Another hypothesis is that perhaps he was a soldier in some special unit," he continued undaunted. "In support of this, there's the fact that he's very tall and has quick reflexes."

Until that moment, Matilde had been holding her breath. Now she let it out slowly, telling herself that she had lost way too much time with Mariano Pizzoccheri. She slowed down her pace.

"Therefore," he went on, "they just need to have a look at all the twenty-two-caliber guns circulating in the city."

"What if the gun came from somewhere else?" Matilde asked. "Why do they keep thinking it's one of us? After all, does it seem credible to you that a murderer would use a registered gun?"

"Ah." Pizzoccheri looked at Matilde as though he had caught her red-handed. "We're talking about a lunatic, not a normal person. A lunatic doesn't stop to consider danger. He courts it. Do you want to know something else? In my opinion, that man frequents some firing range in complete tranquility. No one can shoot that well if he doesn't keep in practice."

Matilde stopped at this point, freeing her arm. When she wanted to, she knew how to be extremely assertive. "Thank you for the company, but now I really must go," she said firmly. "Goodbye."

She left him baffled, right where he was standing, and he watched as she turned toward San Domenico.

As soon as she arrived back home, Matilde went to sit in the old leather easy chair in front of the window in Nanni's study. Some time ago she had definitively abandoned the small chair in the sitting room off her bedroom where she used to record the household expenses or write down the estimates for the maintenance jobs performed at some of the houses she owned. Sometimes she would check the accounts of debits and credits incurred with the manager of the Impruneta house, or even just read the newspapers.

At one time, it seemed ages ago, her husband's study was the room Enea liked best. He used to spend hours and hours taking the books down from the bookcases and weighing them in his hands, as if by doing so he could judge their content. He moved them

54

around according to a system that was all his own. Considering how much time he took for each volume, it must have required a lot of thought. Then he had asked Matilde if he could have his father's books as his own. Matilde was sure Enea had probably read all of them, even studied some of them (absorbed was the word that came to mind when she saw her son bent over the pages). So the question had surprised her.

She had told him yes, and that day he had started dividing the books up all over again, and pasted bookplates in many of them. The labels were kept in a closed, gray cardboard box—little rectangles of paper with an ivory background and sepia-colored design— that he had brought home a few weeks earlier. The design showed a man with his mouth open wide in a scream (Munch, Matilde had thought), and a long, pointed knife aimed at his throat (certainly a touch of Enea's caprice). The books with the labels had been moved to the upstairs floor, and now there were large gaping spaces on the shelves, like missing teeth.

Matilde sat stiffly with her eyes closed, holding her head erect and barely touching the back of the chair. Just a shred of conversation from the annoying encounter with Mariano Pizzoccheri had stuck in her mind. Pizzoccheri had said that the murderer could have learned to shoot while serving in the military. Enea had not done his military service because he was exempted for medical reasons. The old insurance agent had also mentioned the possibility that the man might go to a firing range.

Enea had always been a good shot. He had learned as a boy, first with Nanni, and then later with the estate manager, who in those days was the father of the current manager. He shot better than anyone else, hitting the heart of the targets driven into the trunks of the oak trees without fail. Matilde could still see him—utterly serious with his arm straight out, taking aim and firing the shots. Then he would turn around with his face frowning as he waited for them to tell him how good he had been.

Nanni had gotten little satisfaction from that son, who possessed a mind so similar to his but an awkward and clumsy body. Despite being a doctor, he had noticed the problems that prevented Enea from growing normally too late. When he had finally intervened he was only able to prevent him from getting worse. Having to be satisfied with what his son could offer him, he had boasted enormously about his shooting skills and had pushed him to go to the firing range. As usual, Enea had listened to him. However, one day he had confessed to his father that he did not get any pleasure out of it. In fact, shooting as well as he did made him suspect he was beneath other people. If someone had the capacity for emotions and reactions, he had said, as was natural in all human beings, certainly he could not just stand there with his arm still and his eyes riveted on the target like a tin soldier. Furthermore, hitting a target gave an entirely sterile sense of satisfaction. It would have been different if he had had a person in flesh and blood standing in front of him.

That Enea had always excelled in his studies had been taken for granted by the family. All of them had graduated well ahead of schedule, and they boasted several chairs at the university, and even quite a few historic publications, some of which were very important.

8

"Come on! Come on, say yes!" Nanda pleaded on the telephone. "What do you have to lose? I've got the money. I'll come over to your place."

"The shop is closed these days," answered the pusher.

"I'll even come inside your place. You don't even have to move. Just one fix. What's one fix to you? Then I'll hunt around all over the place. You'll see, I'll find the rest."

"It's no use coming over, because my house is clean. So long."

"Wait, wait, don't hang up. I'll do what you want. I'll do whatever you want."

"You don't do anything for me! A woman like you, well, doesn't even exist for me."

"You piece of shit."

"You're the piece of shit. Speaking of shit, why don't you have that big ox that slobbers all over you get you the dope? If you see him, tell him that one day or another I'll make him pay for that shaking the other night."

The line went dead in Nanda's hand.

For the first time she wondered about Enea. She had never asked herself what kind of feeling tied her to that man. She was not the type to do so, and didn't think it was important either. When she had met him, she had simply sensed that he would get her out of the scrape she was in, letting her have a few days of peace. She had told him the story about the father and the rape because it had worked with other guys. To get people to help you, you have to give them justifications that are out of the ordinary and preferably get on the dirty side. She had two or three of those little tales, tailored to whoever was there to listen to her. Most of the time they had gotten her a bit of cash and a sympathetic look. When things had gone really well, she even had a couple of stays in the hospital that she used to catch her breath, ready to start all over again as soon as she was released. With women, the story that worked was about the daughter left living all alone in an old farmhouse after Nanda's mother, a countrywoman, had recently died, crushed by a tractor. With men, the story about the violent father was the one that had the greatest effect most often.

Enea would have swallowed it too, if Aldo had not shown her to be a liar.

Nanda had thought of Enea as another one of her chance encounters in the beginning and had planned on paying the inevitable price sooner or later. She had happened to make love with some filthy men, and to end up in bed with that old pushover hardly bothered her at all. Instead, Enea had never asked her for anything. In fact, it seemed as if by letting him help her she was doing him a favor.

When she had sat on his knees, determined to repay him in some way, and had discovered his difficulty, she had experienced an unfamiliar feeling, something hovering between disorientation and tenderness. Enea was impotent, but the expression of extreme bliss all over his face when he touched her or gave her some kind of pleasure had deeply upset her. Since then, every time she had done it again, it had been to confirm the unexpected power that he made her aware of—more gratifying than any other feeling. At that point, after she had kept to herself, telling him the first phony story that flew into her head just to get rid of him, Nanda decided to spare him the most unpleasant details, almost out of a sort of sudden respect.

If he arrived with money, fine, and if not, her needs drove her out of the house and she went to get it herself. Their agreement was clear on this point at least, even if no one had said as much. Nevertheless, Nanda had the feeling at times that it was only clear for her. Enea continued to talk about getting her away from that life, to save her from herself and from the vultures, as he called them. He did not ask himself if the concept of salvation had the same meaning for her. This was perhaps the only thing that irritated Nanda, not being able to convince him that she had chosen her life and it was just fine for her as it was. So long as she had her fix of heroin she did not want anything else. If she had to fly around the city like a crazed nocturnal bird in order to get it, that was fine with her too.

Since she still possessed a shadow of sensitivity, Nanda was aware that she had to offer Enea something more than a few caresses. This was especially so whenever he made it possible for her to stay peacefully at home, with the little packet already waiting in the drawer, and not have to get up and set out on her search as the streets beyond the windows disappeared, swallowed by darkness. So she injected the dope in time so that he would not find her with her head lolling around and her eyes blank. She even took a shower to wash off the sour smell she always had.

She didn't know if Enea was independently wealthy or if he picked up cash through some more-or-less legitimate expedients too. She certainly had never forced him to do anything. After all, he was fully grown, big, and even adult enough to act on his own account. Enea had talked to her about his job at Colamele's office, but had not explained whether he was a partner in the agency or something else. Nanda was inclined to believe the first hypothesis, since he was obviously a gentleman. On the other hand, she told herself, if he were a partner in that kind of a notary office, he would not have had the problems with money that periodically afflicted him.

She had never approached Enea in the neighborhood where he worked. She had gone just a few times to wait for him at the corner of via Arte della Lana. Without letting him see her, she had followed him as he walked along absorbed in thought, taking those long strides, each of which cost her three of her own. When she thought that they were far enough away from downtown so she could join him without causing him any embarrassment, she would run up to him and take his arm. He would burst out laughing, as she had seen him do only a few times since she had known him.

That morning though, Nanda decided that she had to go find him, and in a hurry. She felt the monkey creeping up on her and she was at her wits' end. The money was there. She had moved early on it, but she couldn't find any dope. He really had to give her a hand.

Enea was standing behind Andreino Colamele, who was rustling the pages of the deed for a complex transfer of property that involved several apartment houses and pieces of land. To hear his mother talk, when the notary was young, he was famous for his beautiful hands, which he would flutter through the air so everyone could admire them, and for his straight, agile build, like an Olympic athlete's. Now though, Colamele's hands had huge knuckles, twisted by arthritis, and his back was curved. His hair, which had been thick and shiny, was pasted to his head and separated into white clumps stained with a dark yellowish cast. Enea had never been able to imagine Andreino Colamele as ever being handsome and agile. He just thought that if his mother was not exaggerating, then it was better to have never been beautiful than to see oneself reduced to that state in old age.

As the notary closed the blue folder to give it back to Enea with a nod of approval, the office door opened a crack, and the head secretary stuck her head in asking if she could please come in. At Colamele's "please do" she walked straight up to the long, black, claw-footed table, and looked at the notary with the air of a person who has to deliver bothersome news and does not have the courage to do so.

"A telephone call for Doctor Monterispoli," she said contritely. "I brought it to the person's attention that the doctor was busy with the notary, but the woman insists on speaking to him."

"It must be Matilde," suggested Colamele quizzically, as he looked at Enea.

Even though she had never called him at the office, Enea knew for certain that it was Nanda. "I don't know . . . Yes, maybe it's my mother," he hastily answered. Excusing himself, he ran to his office. When he picked up the phone, Nanda sounded upset and told him that she had to see him right away. She was in the café downstairs, and she couldn't take it anymore. If he didn't help her she'd slit her wrists.

"Don't worry, I'm coming down," said Enea, over-wrought. "Don't do anything foolish. Just a moment to lock up my desk and I'll be right there." He spoke loudly, without noticing the head secretary who was standing in the middle of the doorway and openly scrutinizing him.

"Nothing serious, I hope," the woman said in a saccharine voice, as he took his raincoat off the coat rack and slipped through the door.

Taken aback, Enea stopped for a moment, searching for something to say to remedy the situation. "No, no, thanks. It's just that my mother is home with a broken pipe and doesn't know what to do."

"Oh, listen," said the secretary. "I didn't recognize her voice. Give her my best, please."

Nanda was waiting for him inside the main door, and Enea had never seen her in that state. Her features were sharp and she had a piercing look on her face.

"No one is around anymore, they've all disappeared," she immediately assailed him, grabbing onto the collar of his raincoat. "I managed to find one of them, just one of those bastards. He won't cough it up." She continued talking, now clutching Enea's arm, while he dragged her along toward the Mercato Nuovo. Despite the cold weather, the tourist season had already begun. The streets were crowded with people who blocked the sidewalks, making it impossible to walk fast.

"There are police everywhere," shrieked Nanda, "all because of that piece of shit who's going around killing people. As if we had anything to do with it. Anyhow, the fact is that you can't find dope anywhere around here at all."

"Shhh!" Enea said, seeing a few passersby turn around, hearing her talk so loudly.

The young woman had almost all of her weight on him and was shaking from head to toe not because she was in withdrawal, but because she was worried about being left without any heroin. She was aware of that, but couldn't do anything about it. Enea continued to walk, frowning, unable to make a decision. Nanda was the one who suggested something to him.

"We have to go out of town," she said. "To Prato, maybe, or Pistoia. Do you have a car? If we go by car it won't take us long. Straight there and straight back."

It suddenly dawned on Enea that if he were to help Nanda in that moment, he would never be able to refuse anything she asked him in the future. He fleetingly thought of making up a story about car trouble, but Nanda seemed to anticipate his refusal. She started saying again that she would slit her wrists, she might as well end it all. Instead of killing innocent young people, it would be better for the Monster to kill her.

"Relax, relax," Enea said softly. "We'll take care of it somehow, you'll see. But you have to promise me you'll help me find a more permanent solution, afterwards."

Nanda kept nodding her head yes, until he finally said that he would get the car and then come by to pick her up on via de' Renai, and she had to go wait for him there.

"Who's going to guarantee that you won't disappear then? I'm coming with you." She flew into a fit. Her voice turned shrill and her head shook as if she were having convulsions. "I'm coming with you, I'm telling you. I'll stay calm. I won't let anyone see me. But I'm coming with you."

Enea didn't feel like going all the way home, thinking about all of the explanations he would have to give his mother. He decided to see if George Lockridge was in his shop. He always kept a small, yellow, two-horsepower car in front that he used in the evening to go back to the farmhouse where he lived. If George was there, he would have him lend it to him.

George was there, and he lent him the car.

9

Winter had come and gone, leaving the city numbed with cold and the olive trees frozen on the hillsides. Matilde had spent that time of the year as she had spent all of those before it. She left the house around ten o'clock in the morning, muffled up in her old Persian lamb fur coat and a wool scarf protecting her head, and went for long walks that most of the time took her to the school of music and beyond. She never had her fill of the beauty of the hillside that rose gently from the north of the city reaching up to Fiesole. If she went by Piazza San Domenico, she would stop to look at the elegant portico of the church and the little bell tower. Or if she happened to pass by via dei Roccettini, she went the long way around so she could become lost in admiring the austere facade of the Badia Fiesolana church.

People often complimented her on her youthful appearance. Matilde replied that if everyone had walked as much as she did, they would have been better off. She did not wonder whether the compliment was sincere, because she knew she still had smooth, glowing skin. Though in the last few months, the image staring back at her from the mirror had started to show sagging cheeks and a mouth marked suddenly by signs of hidden suffering.

Spring had now begun to warm the days. The time had arrived to run out to Impruneta to air out the house and go over the accounts with the estate manager. One morning Matilde let her son know about her intention to go up to the country house.

"I'll try to find the time to take you," replied Enea.

Matilde could barely keep herself from retorting that since he only worked a half-day after reducing his schedule, it was hard to understand how in the world he would not be able to take her there, even right away.

"You need to make an effort," she said instead. "With the cold weather we've had, everything will be damp, including the furniture, the paintings, and all the rest of the things. I bet that Angiolina didn't open the windows even once this winter."

She would also make use of the trip to the Impruneta house to do some inventory of the items that she had in the house and other things on the property. One evening, when she had invited Andreino Colamele and a couple of doctors who had been her husband's colleagues over to dinner, she had gone straight to the dining room buffet to get out a vegetable dish, but it was not there. She had called Saveria and showered her with a torrent of words that, if lined up and reordered according to what Matilde intended, laid the responsibility on the other woman.

"It was a valuable piece. The kind that antique dealers display on velvet," she said resentfully.

Saveria replied that she didn't know what vegetable dish she was talking about. Matilde explained, describing it to her down to the last detail. "It was from the eighteenth century, if you really want to know. A French design made in Faenza, with a splendid blue pattern."

The relationship that existed between the two women had lasted over twenty years and was guided by a rigid code of behavior, according to which Matilde was the mistress of the house and Saveria was the servant. Therefore, Matilde had the right to go beyond her usual moderation and express herself with a certain forcefulness. Left all alone after the death of her husband, Saveria had been uprooted from the region of Basilicata by her two children, who had started their own families in Florence. Still too young not to work and too proud to have others support her, she had heard about a lady looking for a housekeeper to work days full-time. She had shown up at the house in San Domenico to apply for the job, just as she was, without ever having worked in someone's service and without any references. Matilde had had her leave her name and address. Even though her keen nose convinced her a stroke of luck had come her way, she had made inquiries about the woman and about her children through friends of her brother-in-law, Dono, at police headquarters. In the end, Matilde had hired her.

Matilde and Saveria spoke to each other using very polite forms of address that were customary years ago. This contributed to the development of a special relationship between them that sometimes bordered on complicity. But not the day of the vegetable dish incident.

"Don't pretend you don't remember it," said Matilde resolutely. "You know full well what I am talking about." Not daring to spell out her suspicion, which she felt was nonetheless sacrosanct and justified, she added, "Maybe you broke it and don't have the nerve to admit it."

Enea had to intervene, drawn by the voices that rose from the kitchen. He tried to calm down his mother and also Saveria, telling them that nothing was ever solved with impetuousness and insisting that the vegetable dish was probably at the Impruneta house together with the other dishes. Matilde yielded, out of fear of losing Saveria more than anything else. Yet she was still convinced that at the very least, the woman had broken the precious dish.

"We'll see," she concluded.

The vegetable dish had been sold by Enea on a day when it was extremely cold, in order to save Nanda, who had a bad cough, from going out of the house. The young woman was in one of her bouts of depression and started threatening to cut her wrists again. Enea had gone to the Englishman's shop to ask him where he could get some money, and George had answered that with all of the treasures that filled his house, he only had to take one of them and bring it to him.

"Certainly there's no time to make copies, seeing the hurry you're in," and he added "Just this once, you only need to choose something from that beautiful china set your mother keeps in the buffet in the dining room."

So Enea brought the vegetable dish to George Lockridge. He made exactly the amount of money he needed from it, not one lira more and not one less, in order to make Nanda calm down for two days and to give himself a little breather too.

That morning, Matilde went over to the calendar that she kept hanging in the kitchen next to the stove, to see if there was some anniversary to remember or some particular purchase to take care of. She always filled in the calendar well before December 31, putting the new one behind the old, so it would be all ready when she needed it. She would always copy the birthdays and anniversaries onto the new calendar, so that she would not run the risk of forgetting one of them. She had already sent flowers to Andreino Colamele's head secretary, who would have her birthday on the twentieth of March, and had given her sister-in-law a hand-embroidered tea doily for her wedding anniversary. In a short while it would be Enea's birthday (his last before crossing the threshold into his fifties), and Matilde thought she would order the volumes from Pléiade in Paris. He said he wanted to try and acquire them, but had not found the time yet. While she ran her eyes over the days of the month, she noticed that there was a new moon that night. There had been other nights with a new moon during the eight months that had passed since the last double homicide, but it seemed to Matilde that this one had special significance. She stood there staring at the calendar for a few minutes, as if she were reading an omen, then she shook herself out of it. She informed Saveria that she was going out, and kept to her plan to walk as far as the flower market to buy some new plants for the garden.

Matilde stayed up late, and after such a long time of avoiding the sitting room, she went in to sit and watch the television. She had heard Enea leave on his moped, and she felt uneasy. It meant that her son did not know

69

when he would be coming back and whether he would make it in time to catch the last bus. She imagined him riding around the city, bent over the handlebars (but where was he going?), wandering about until he was so tired he would finally make his way back home. Since Matilde could not fathom that someone might ride a moped aimlessly around the streets downtown for hours, she thought that maybe Enea was going beyond the residential area. After she had discovered the case of scalpels out of place and found the police in her own home, she had again promised herself not to shrink from any suppositions, however painful. She forced herself to admit that she could imagine Enea going around clearings and thickets on the outskirts of the city. To "scout the areas," as the newspapers had written.

When she went to bed it was past one. She lay awake looking at the dim light that she had left on in the sitting room until she heard her son arrive. She recognized the sound of the motor as it came closer and died out, and finally the footsteps and the tires dragging across the gravel in the garden. If he came home particularly late, Enea got off the moped at the corner of the house and then pushed it with his strong arms all the way into the garage. The rolling metal shutter rattled on its tracks as it was raised and then lowered again. The footsteps went along the narrow sidewalk in front of the kitchen, came inside, and moved away toward the bedroom and the bath. After a few minutes, they came back into the hallway, followed after the creaking door, and went upstairs to the study. Matilde expected to hear the shoes being placed softly on the wood floor, to be exchanged for the slippers, but it did not happen. Enea was not moving up there. What was he doing?

She lifted her head off the pillow, craning it toward the ceiling in order to make sure that the silence was really silence. The silence was so deep that for an instant she seemed to hear her son's labored breathing, as if he were crying.

10

The Volkswagen van is equipped as a camper. Its lights are on, and obsessive rock music blares from the radio at full blast, streaming into the darkness during the new moon. The tall wall bordering the park at the villa is covered with moss. Large tree branches reach up to the top of the wall and hang down the other side, almost touching the roof of the camper parked in the open space a few meters from the road.

Two people inside. One of them has long blond hair and is lying face down, forehead resting on a folded arm, the body partially hidden by a sleeping bag. The person is dozing, with legs pointed toward the back of the vehicle and head toward the dashboard. Beside the prone body is a young man wearing only bikini briefs, sitting on the floor with his shoulder leaning against a small cabinet. His naked legs are crossed on top of the sleeping bag. He is reading a magazine and keeping time to the music with his toes.

Outside, the man presses up against the wall and looks at the bright windows, which stand out in the night like pictures hanging in the darkness. The blasts of rock music reach him, screaming at him that inside, there are some young people.

He advances cautiously, his long arms dangling,

flattens himself up against the side of the camper, and spies inside. He sees the young man who is reading and sees the body with the long blond hair. He takes out his gun, moves half a step, turns, and shoots through the window. The bullets hit the head of the person lying down, then the back and the liver.

The man notices that the young man in his underwear, terrorized, jumps and dives into the back of the camper, crouching in the corner on the same side he's on. He can't see him anymore. He moves, circling around the trunk of the vehicle in a few quick leaps. He reaches the window on the other side, puts the mouth of the gun against the glass, and shoots. The bullet strikes the young man in the jaw.

The man throws open the door and jumps, bursting into the camper. He approaches the young man, who is screaming and trying to protect his bloody face, covering it up with his hands. The man shoots again, straight at the mouth, the bullet passing through his hand, then his thigh. It seems as if he doesn't want to leave anything intact.

He puts the gun in his pocket, takes out the sharp knife. He slowly bends over to grab the blond head by the hair and turns it around. This one is a male too.

The man lets go, uncertain for an instant, and looks around, his head moving fitfully. He sees the magazine on the floor and bends over to pick it up. It's written in German. The pictures show scenes of lovemaking between two gay men.

The man turns around like a madman, waving the magazine in the air, and runs out of the camper. He furiously rips up the pages, reducing them to tiny little shreds, and scatters them all around.

He runs away into the night, enormous, clumsy, disappointed.

The morning after the new moon, Matilde turned on the radio, but she did not hear what she feared. She turned it on in the afternoon too, and then in the evening, she listened to the television. The next day, she went through the same three motions again, waiting and holding her breath, her mouth shut. She finally heaved a sigh of relief. It seemed that nothing had really happened.

Early the third morning, Enea made up his mind to take her to the house at Impruneta. For a while, Matilde did not have either the time or desire to listen to the radio or the television, or even to read the newspapers. She thus spared herself finding out right away that two young Germans had been killed, taken by surprise in a camper parked in a clearing near the area of Galluzzo. The bodies had been found after two days, and the news was reported on the third day.

Matilde was staying at the old villa and made arrangements with her son to pick her up the following Saturday. The house was very large, painted in the same soft yellow as the San Domenico home. A veranda ran along one side of the villa, and the view of the front was broken up by a portico supported by columns and embellished with four medallions made of multicolored terracotta. From the terrace on the second floor, one could see the Greve River, which flowed less than three hundred yards away, and the tall bell tower of Santa Maria Impruneta. Otherwise, the green of holms and a variety of other oaks was unbroken.

The first thing Matilde did was summon Angiolina,

the estate manager's wife, so that she could help her open the windows and vacuum all of the rooms. She kept the windows wide open to let the sun come inside and take away the stuffy smell permeating the entire house. Thanks to the sturdy framing and the impermeable, thick walls, the winter had not caused any damage. The air inside was freezing though, and the cold continued to linger despite the warmth outside, and the couches felt as if they were damp. Matilde did not even put the kitchen in running order, except what was necessary for making coffee. She had her meals in a restaurant owned by a godson of hers, just a few hundred yards from the gate on the road to Grassina. In the evening she had a fire lit in the fireplace in her bedroom.

The second morning at Impruneta, she woke up with the vegetable dish on her mind and wanted to see if it was really there as Enea had suggested. She barely had time to slip into her robe before she heard Angiolina below the windows talking with Jacopo, the baker woman's grandson. He stopped in every day to drop off the bread on his way to deliver supplies to the American college at the top of the hillside.

"They ought to shoot him down like a dog," Angiolina was saying. "A creature like that doesn't deserve any mercy. What harm were they doing, those two poor kids?"

"I don't know about harm," replied Jacopo, who was a big young fellow, with a slow wit but a fast tongue. "I only know that they weren't that normal. Didn't you hear about it on television? They were queers." And he laughed. "Not even the Monster liked them. So much so, he didn't think they were worth cutting even once."

Matilde appeared at the window, asking loudly, "What are you two saying? What are you talking about? Do you mind telling me how it is that you always have some morsel of news to share?"

Before she even heard from Angiolina that two young men had been killed, Matilde already knew what had happened.

She forgot to check on the vegetable dish.

ᦏᧈ

Saturday morning, Matilde went through the whole house to close up all of the shutters and the windows, leaving her bedroom till last. She had already put all of her things back in her small suitcase and was waiting for Enea to take her back to Florence. Until he arrived, she would enjoy the last rays of sunshine at Impruneta sitting on the stone bench at the back of the garden. Two things happened that prevented her from leaving at the arranged time.

Enea called to tell her that he had not been well. His voice was weak, and it was hard for him to talk. Matilde had to press him to find out what had happened. Her son finally brought himself to confess that he had had an attack of hypoglycemia. Fortunately it had happened while he was in the office. They had taken him to the emergency room at the hospital, where they had called Uncle Dono's department. Then he had rushed down together with Doctor Morigi. Nothing that could not be remedied. They had said that his diabetes was acting up, and it was necessary to keep an eye on it. The only treatment, besides insulin, was a special diet. He also had to change the type of insulin. The slow acting insulin wasn't strong enough anymore, and he needed to use the semi-slow.

CRCRCR CRCRCR CRCRCR

"Goodness knows how you've let yourself go these days," Matilde grumbled. She was about to add that good health must be earned, but held herself back. Enea seemed desolate. She felt a prick of discomfort at the idea of having left him alone all those days. "Enea, you ought to . . ."

"Mama, please," he interrupted her. "Do you want me to send someone to pick you up? Or will you stay there until I feel better, and then I'll come up?"

"Don't worry about it," answered Matilde. "I'll find a way to get back home, even if I have to take the bus."

Enea tried to convince her that staying a few days at Impruneta could only do her good, but she preferred to put off making any decisions. If her conscience had not told her to return home to her son, Matilde actually would have stayed over. The thin air at Impruneta gave her a pleasant giddy sensation, and the expanse of holm oaks that covered the hillside gave off a good country smell. The location of the house, high up in the small valley, had always given her a priceless feeling of space that she had never experienced in the city. Up there, her anxieties dissipated, and the ghosts that assailed her thoughts in Florence grew distant.

She started to fiddle with the buckle on her suitcase, uncertain about whether she should take her things out and actually push her departure back a few days. Suddenly she heard feet running loudly under the window, and Angiolina was yelling, "My goodness! Oh my goodness!" Antonella, the daughter of Angiolina's daughter, a sweet little six-year-old girl who never stood still, had gotten an ugly cut on her leg. She had fallen off a ladder onto a scythe in the orchard. She had to be taken to the hospital, and Matilde could tell from the way Angiolina was looking at her that she expected to see her come with them, since she knew all of the doctors and was treated with high regard.

It was almost dinnertime when they returned, and Matilde thought she would ask the estate manager to take her straight to Florence. But when they arrived at the villa, there was a yellow car in the space on the side of the house that was bordered by a myrtle hedge. The car door was open and an old man sat in the driver's seat with his feet on the footboard, staring blankly into space.

Matilde said goodbye to Angiolina's daughter, thanking her for the ride back to her house, and went over to the car to ask the man what he wanted. But he did not give her time to open her mouth. He stood up and went toward her with outstretched arms.

"Dear Matilde, I'm finally seeing you again!" he said, his voice shaking too much even for an old man like him. "Do you know you haven't changed at all? I hope you're as happy as I am about this opportunity that has brought us together again after all these years."

Matilde was dumbstruck, trying her utmost to remember who it could be. She looked closely at his purplish face, the fine white hair hanging down to his shoulders, the big red shirt, too roomy for his shrunken body. It was impossible to see his eyes, hidden as they were behind the thick lenses of his glasses.

The old man started to shake his head and moan. "I knew you wouldn't recognize me. I must really have become a wreck." He hid his face behind his hands, but then he smiled. "But you, on the other hand. How have you kept yourself looking like that? I know, I know, you're a lot younger than I am. Even so, you still look extraordinary. It really must be said that art illuminates the mind but doesn't help to keep the body in shape."

"George?" hazarded Matilde, uncertain. The last time they had met, the Englishman still spoke Italian haltingly, choosing his words one by one and stumbling over the pronunciation. However, aside from a slight trace of a foreign accent, the old man had the smooth way of speaking typical of the people living in the area.

"It's really me, George, in flesh and bones . . . Oh God, let's say more bones than flesh." He held out his arms again, but Matilde ignored the invitation and proposed he come inside, asking him if he wanted some coffee. When George answered that he would gladly have some, they moved into the spacious, vaulted ceiling kitchen. Other than the electric stove and the refrigerator, the kitchen looked as if it had remained the same since the villa had been built over five hundred years before.

Matilde laid a small white tablecloth with red flowers on a corner of the marble table and apologized for not having anything else to offer him.

"I was about to return to Florence," she said. "Enea was supposed to pick me up, but he hasn't been well."

Not knowing whether her son might have told her that they had seen each other, George kept on the vague side. "How is dear Enea?"

"Not that well," repeated Matilde evasively. From the moment she had recognized George, she kept wondering how he had known that she was there and why in the world he had come. When it seemed opportune to ask him, she did, in the voice she used if something did not appear clear to her.

George laughed. "I was simply passing by this way and the windows were open. Ah, Matilde, I see you still haven't lost the habit of viewing everything and everyone with suspicion. But the responsibility is ours, the group from the old days, I mean. You were there listening to the discussions and malicious talk we cooked up in a constant stream, and you soaked it all up like a small thirsty sponge. We boasted about wanting to reform the world. In reality, we were simply giving vent to our twisted feelings of revenge, to our petty miseries. I was supposed to vindicate my being different. Nanni was supposed to make amends for being wealthy. Andreino was just waiting for an opening he could slip into so he could deposit his eggs as a little social climber. And your brother-in-law, Dono, got drunk on the scents wafting from your young body. He went crazy with jealousy because Nanni was the one who would savor it at night." He sniggered, shaking his head as if the image of those days were really before his eyes.

Matilde felt extremely uncomfortable. The Englishman told only a part of the truth, and in an entirely partial way. She preserved something very different in her memory as the true meaning of those meetings in her home. She remembered the languishing looks cast by her brother-in-law's glances, the acute awareness of her own body that the presence of all of those men gave her, and Nanni's deep, ironic look. He understood, and enjoyed it. In those days, her cheeks always burned with a secret excitement.

She changed the subject, asking George what line of work he was in and if he still painted those beautiful landscapes veiled in mist, a mingling of the Tuscan countryside and homesickness for the fogs of England.

"No, no," he answered. "Woe betide the artist who comes to a standstill with formal solutions that remain immutable over time. If I had continued to paint those landscapes, I would have become crystallized in an unreal vision of the world. Can you imagine my landscapes, in these times? No, no. But anyway, after discovering I wasn't the master I thought I was, and not knowing how to revive my palette, today I work in restoration. I get pleasure out of giving color and form back to antique works of art that have lost their splendor out of neglect or by chance."

In other words, George frittered away his entire day touching up old daubs of no value, thought Matilde. She had always been bothered by people she defined as "the poor." For her, poverty was more of a mental category than an economic one. Her poor people were those who in some way possessed the kind of culture and manners that could have put them among the rich, but they were afflicted by a congenital sense of inferiority and the inability to transform their talents into riches, always remaining in the middle of the road, with no precise place. They winked at the people who were actually poor, implying that they were joined by the same bad fortune, lacking money for sure, but certainly not inferior to the others as far as acumen or intelligence were concerned. They winked at the rich too, pretending to know and apply their same rules of savoir faire, the only rules able to distinguish them from the poor.

The trees were disappearing outside, swallowed by the setting sun. Matilde started to feel ill-at-ease over not having decided yet whether to stay at Impruneta or return home. She removed the coffee cups and put them in the stone grit sink, turning around to look at the Englishman with a politely questioning expression. George Lockridge got the message, but did not give up. He had heard from Enea that Matilde had gone up to the Impruneta house, and he had caught up with her, firmly convinced that he could not let an opportunity like that escape him.

He remembered every one of the paintings and every one of the beautiful pieces in the home with extreme precision. Nonetheless, it was important for him to see them again. If he had to guide Enea in the choice of something in particular in the future, it was better to refresh his memory.

"You want to go back home, don't you?" he asked Matilde. "If you do me this honor, I'll drive you back. Right up to your doorstep." He hesitated, sighing, and let his eyes wander beyond the French window in the kitchen toward the garden. "I don't dare ask you," he said then, injecting a hesitant tone into his voice, "but since I'm here, and who knows how many more years will go by before I come back, supposing that I might return, would you again take me to see the rooms and paintings that fed my youthful hunger for beauty when I, a penniless dreamer, used to come here to drink up the art?"

Matilde, who was normally annoyed by the shameless rhetoric with which the Englishman flowered his conversation, was touched by that request. She accompanied him on his *recherche* (as he defined it), and was hardly surprised when the painter wanted to linger in the gallery, as he called Nanni's collection of paintings.

"Do you remember this one?" asked George, standing in front of the Rosai. He had taken off his glasses and his nose was nearly glued to the canvas. "Splendid. Splendid. Do you remember that I was the one who kept insisting that Nanni buy it from the heirs of that broker from Compiobbi? They didn't even know what they had right in their hands, and he carried it off for a song."

Matilde said that yes, she remembered, even though it was not true. George thought that if it had gone so well with the Rosai, it would go fine with the rest.

II

When she returned to Florence and discovered that the entire city was still talking about the last double murder, Matilde was swept up in the collective curiosity and started avidly reading all of the newspapers. She even went so far as to buy some of the scandalmongering magazines that she had not even imagined existed. The mere reference to the killer on a cover or in a headline gave her an irresistible urge to find out what they said.

She ultimately felt reassured. Maybe the visit from the police, which had started so many ugly thoughts churning inside her, had been prompted by their overzealousness. The case of scalpels that was out of place, to which she had attributed such dark meanings, in all probability had been her own doing in a moment of distraction.

While Enea continued his usual life, running all over the city looking for Nanda or the Englishman or the pusher (by now the young woman sent him to buy the dope, with the excuse that she didn't want to see those scoundrels anymore), Matilde attended to the garden and the orchard.

Even though her son could not eat preserves, and she barely even touched them herself, when the moment

84

arrived to gather the fruit from the trees behind the house, she collected the jars left over from the year before, which sat in a row on the top shelf of the cupboard. Carefully arranging the preserves in a big basket, she told Saveria to ask her children to come and take them again, with a reminder to put aside the empty jars for the next year. Then she would again begin to peel the fruit and prepare syrups and write labels with the date and the contents of each jar.

She had also started going to the dinners at the Badia Fiesolana again, on the first Friday of the month. They were open to anyone who wanted to attend, and everyone brought something to eat. Before the service in the chapel, the women in the neighborhood generally arrived with pies and cakes that were set out on a table against the wall of the refectory.

As always in August, Matilde and Enea would have to go to Viareggio for a few weeks, to their small villa on the sea. Like the Impruneta house, the villa had to be opened up, if for no other reason than to air the furniture and rooms. Enea had already started to put up some resistance, maintaining that in the months when the office was less busy with clients, he should finish the backlog of work. Besides that, the library would stay open the entire month of August that year, and he would take advantage of it to do some research of his on the developments of romanticism in Bohemia. There had been other times before when Enea had said he did not want to go to Viareggio, but he had always changed his mind. So Matilde did not worry about it.

Already since June, Nanda had shown signs of being on edge. In the summer it was difficult to find dope, and the little that was around was horrible. Everyone moved to the seashore or the mountains, and she would also be forced to go someplace with her friends.

If someone had told Enea that his relationship with Nanda closely resembled an anxious mother's, he would have shaken his head, incredulous, convinced as he was that he was firmly leading the young woman toward an impending resurrection. He was becoming increasingly aware of the difficulties, but remained resolutely convinced of the final results. On the other hand, Nanda's company had become so essential to him that he could not even imagine his own existence without her.

When the first Florentines began leaving the city for their vacations, Nanda did not hide her restlessness. She disappeared for hours and complained about having to stay cooped up inside those four walls. If she saw Enea frown, she changed her tone and jumped on his knees, again starting up the games that sent him into ecstasy. They were always the same, because Nanda had neither the desire nor the imagination to change them. In any case, he did not seem to ask for anything else.

One night, driven by more acute anxiety than usual, Enea stole out of the house like a thief and went down to via de' Renai to look for her. She was not there. He stayed to wait, sitting on the sidewalk until dawn. When he saw her appear at the end of the street, with that easygoing walk of hers that made her recognizable even at a distance, he was seized by a sense of relief and anger all at once.

"Where have you been? Aren't you going to tell me where you've been?" he asked, rising up before her when she arrived in front of him.

Nanda drew back, frightened. Then she recognized him and laughed nervously. "What are you doing here at this hour?"

"Where have you been?" Enea repeated.

"Out. I felt like I was suffocating, stuck at home." Then she saw his expression and started to talk faster and faster. "I didn't do anything wrong. I was walking around, I met a couple of friends. I came back. Nothing wrong, do you understand? And if you don't believe me, too bad for you. Trust—either it's there or it's not. Do I ever ask you where you've been?"

Another time, Nanda ran out of money faster than expected. Enea was desperate because he had just sold a sketch by Domenico Morelli and did not know how to get more cash in a hurry.

"But what did you do with all of it? Can you tell me what you did with it?" he asked, shaking his head back and forth, as if he had something inside that he was trying to get out.

"I used it for a good cause," said Nanda. "If that's not okay with you, I don't want to see you anymore."

"What good cause?" insisted Enea.

Nanda got up off the easy chair she had been curled up in and began wandering around the room. "The mother of a friend of mine is dying. As if that weren't enough, my friend was fired on the spot. She goes nights without sleeping so she can look after that poor wretch, and her boss kicked her out because she always came in late in the morning. Does that seem decent?"

In reality, Nanda needed more fixes. Besides that, she had met a young guy who wormed money out of her.

"Anyhow, if you don't have a heart, that's your business," she continued, worried by Enea's silence. She went up to him, took his chin in her hand, and made him look at her. "Do you want me to get mad? Do you want me to get mad, or do you want me to caress you a little instead?"

Since he would not answer, she added, "Actually, no. Today I'm not going to caress you. Today I'm going to teach you something instead."

She started to get undressed, tossing her clothes in a corner.

"I know you're curious about it. I know you still don't know what it looks like." She pulled a chair up in front of Enea, sat down, grabbed her knees with her arms, pulled up her legs, and opened them. "Do you like it? Do you like it, Enea?"

Enea sat as if he were petrified. He squinted his eyes, holding out the palms of his hands.

"Come on, look! That way you'll understand what I feel when you touch me."

Nanda would not stop talking, so Enea jumped up to cover her mouth with his hand. Then he looked her in the face, lifted her up and threw her on the bed, falling on top of her like a rock. He touched her convulsively, hurting her, lifting her up, and letting her fall back down on the mattress, rubbing his face against her breasts. At the moment when Nanda was saying "yes, yes, Enea, like that," he suddenly drew back, got up and ran out of the room with a long sob.

⟳

Around that time Matilde went to dinner at the Sensinis', who were celebrating their silver wedding anniversary. The Sensinis, Timoteo and Calambrina, were the only friends that she had not inherited from Nanni.

She had met Calambrina at a ceramics exhibit. The gallery, which must have had her name on its mailing list for who knows how many years, regularly sent her invitations. Even though she was not very fond of events like that, she went that day, partly because she had happened to pass right in front of the gallery and also because she had seen some earthenware in the window that seemed pretty. She had asked if she could buy a tall vase whose classic egg-shaped form and cobalt-blue bottom, spread so thick it seemed in relief, gave it a certain elegance. However, Calambrina, the artist who made the ceramic pieces, was so touched by Matilde's admiration that she insisted on giving it to her as a present. Later on, after exchanging telephone calls, they began seeing each other. They stopped only because Calambrina and her husband moved to Switzerland for a while, when he had taken a position in Italian literature at the University of Berne.

When the Sensinis moved back to Florence, Matilde started seeing them again, although their ties were not as close as before. Calambrina had a way about her that had excited her at first, reminding her somehow of the turmoil at the meetings among Nanni's friends, yet ended up annoying her as time passed. She was almost the same age as Matilde and had a thick braid of salt-and-pepper hair that became frizzy when it hung loose. She never tired of going over the importance of rigorous ethics, for one's own behavior most of all.

Matilde only accepted the invitation to dinner because she was lonely. She certainly did not imagine that that occasion, instead of distracting her, would push her further down the road of torment.

The Sensini home, located on the top floor of a building along the Lungarni, was full of rustic furniture for the most part. The bookshelves overflowed with Calambrina's ceramic works, which also invaded part of the tile floor. Timoteo had a cozy study in which he could barely turn around because he had crammed so many books inside. Yet he only seemed comfortable when he could close himself up in there.

Matilde arrived short of breath after climbing the five flights of stairs, only to discover as soon as the door was opened that she would not enjoy eating the meal. The air was full of the scent of curry, a spice that Calambrina used often and that she detested.

Besides Matilde and the hosts, there were nine people seated for dinner. It took her a while at first to understand that the young couple in blue jeans and cashmere jackets was from Zurich, and the woman with the bluish-hued white hair and her companion were British, just passing through, and owned a gallery in Oxford where Calambrina had exhibited her ceramics. With the others she had less difficulty, since she had met them before. There was the director of the Bank of Buon Suffragio with his wife and daughter, two petite women with the same hairstyle and the same silk outfit. There were also two men who always moved as a pair, both of them financial consultants. They did not share any resemblance. One was wiry and nervous, and the other one seemed to glory in his massive weight, yet they were somehow similar.

From the very beginning, the topic was the Monster. It was as if the get-together had been organized to discuss murders instead of to celebrate the hosts' silver wedding anniversary. Everyone had his own opinion to share. The bank director, a big man with a red face and snow-white hair, informed them in a conspiratorial voice that he had found out from a reliable source that the killer was a well-known doctor in the city who was about to be incriminated at any moment.

"Come off it. Oh come off it," jumped in one of the financial consultants, the slenderer and more aggressive of the two. "That man comes from someplace else. My English friends will forgive me . . ." and he shot a wink at the two gallery owners from Oxford, "but his modus operandi has no parallel in Italian criminology, whereas it has many of them in England's."

As for the two young Swiss people, journalists for German-language television, they maintained they had solid information that the Monster was a pure-blooded Florentine, and what's more, belonged to a very high social class.

"In my opinion," said Calambrina, who had her own way of dominating a conversation, as if she had been used to being in command forever, "he is just some poor guy. He's mentally ill. Didn't you read that he must be suffering from hypergonadism? I can just imagine him, big and tall, uncoordinated, and probably impotent. He roams around the countryside to avoid his fellow human beings. Then when he sees two young people enjoying the pleasures of love as he never could, he loses his head and goes wild. Not that I want to sympathize with him, you understand. But let's really try to understand these things, these kinds of behaviors. If he's ill, he's ill."

At that moment, Matilde felt like she hated her. "Who ever said that he suffers from hypergonadism?" she forced herself to ask, leaning over her plate.

"The newspapers. They said it," answered Calambrina. "Look, they didn't invent it. They simply published the report of an expert criminologist, supported by the opinion of a psychiatrist and a psychologist."

"I don't seem to have read that," Matilde curtly replied.

"You must have missed it," declared Calambrina. "Anyway, they actually want to organize anti-Monster squads and to stop all of the cars traveling in the outskirts. Mark my words, that kind of person goes from place to place on foot. Or at the very least, on a moped or bicycle. He moves like a fish in water on inaccessible routes, so someone would have to travel that way. Otherwise they couldn't be familiar with them at all."

"But if he is big and tall, as they say," interjected the bank director's wife, in a whining, barely audible voice, "how does he manage to stay on a moped?"

"What? Are small people the only ones who ride mopeds? Take Enea, Matilde's son. He rides all over the place on a moped just fine. I don't think the Monster could be any bigger and taller than he is."

Matilde burst out uncontrollably. "Calambrina, stop saying such stupid things!"

Calambrina looked at her, surprised. "But what's gotten into you? Are you annoyed because I mentioned Enea?" She looked at her closely, unable to understand. "But you know how much I love him!"

"Certainly you could have gone without saying it," replied Matilde. From that moment on, she did not open her mouth again.

12

As it turned out, they actually did not go to Viareggio that year. Enea had become obstinate about not budging from Florence and Matilde did not feel like insisting either. Maybe it was better to stay in the city after Enea's sick spell. It could happen again, God forbid. The weather was sweltering. Even in the airy house in San Domenico it was impossible to breathe until the sun went down and all of the windows were opened.

Matilde spent most of the time in front of the television because the sun beat down too fiercely to go out during the daytime, and by evening she felt exhausted from the scorching heat. That was how she happened to see a broadcast on television that recapitulated the acts committed by the killer murdering couples. The relative tranquility she had been lulled into after blanking out the memory of what Calambrina had said suddenly dissolved. The gnawing suspicion started to consume her thoughts again, most of all at night, with constant, intense activity. Lacking new nourishment to feed upon, it coiled around itself and continued to emit its poisons.

Enea, on the other hand, was living through a period of relative serenity. After collapsing from a shot of badly cut heroin, Nanda had been persuaded to enter a clinic. The stifling heat and some problems she had had with her liver had drained all her strength. So she welcomed as a salutary break not having to live with the anguish brought on by the vacation season and the absence of the pushers in the city streets. Enea breathed easier too.

The bills for the clinic, though steep, were nothing compared to the price of several fixes a day. Nanda also seemed truly determined to get out of that ugly scene once and for all. If Enea was able to see a future, he imagined it with a peaceful Nanda, maybe fixed up with him, living in a house somewhere, or else (but he thought this only in moments when he felt old and tired) back living with her husband, who was a good fellow, after all.

If he had had to continue supplying her with money, he would not have known what to do. George Lockridge had disappeared, undoubtedly to go enjoy cool weather somewhere too. Enea did not have any other contacts who could try to sell the paintings at the Impruneta house. He had put aside quite a healthy sum by underselling a *Capriccio* by Guardi, which had been one of the more valuable pieces in the collection, to the Englishman. However, between the rent at via de' Renai, the bills for the clinic, and Nanda's expenses before going to the clinic, he could count on having enough money for six months on his own, more or less.

He went to visit Nanda every afternoon, bringing her a change of clothes and some sweets. He kept telling her he was amazed at how quickly she was recovering. She seemed to blossom again, and her cheeks were brimming with health. Then Nanda got fed up one day, and said to him, "But what do you mean brimming with health! It's puffiness from the sedatives and not taking any dope. When I look at myself in the mirror I'm disgusted. If it weren't for this hot weather wearing me out, I'd be on the streets again."

"Then, you still think about it?"

"Do I think about it? I'll *always* think about it."

Enea had been raised to be discrete, but during those days he discovered a world that he could only define as "secretive." In the clinic, if the nurses had to refer to Nanda's case, they spoke in vague terms of a nervous breakdown, and Aldo Mazzacane pretended to meet him now and again as if it were by chance. (He never called him at home or in the office.) He complained about the hot weather, asked him how he was and when he would go on vacation. Then just at the last moment he asked about Nanda. He felt he had to justify himself all the time, maintaining that her mother, the poor woman, wouldn't leave him in peace if he didn't bring her some news about her daughter. In fact, the woman thanked Enea so much for the interest he'd taken.

One day, Enea arrived to see Nanda with a bouquet of flowers, sat down near the bed, and asked, "Does staying here make you suffer a lot?"

Nanda did not give him a direct answer. "They load me up with sedatives," she said. "So long as you keep paying the bills, they're more than happy to keep me going on Valium and Serenase."

Enea also brought her a few books. He chose them from the ones that were not cataloged yet, but not out of a jealous sense of protection for his personal books. He was sincerely convinced that those titles were more suited to her. After thinking about it a long time, he took *El Señor Presidente* by Miguel Ángel Asturias, believing that she might enjoy the story of Cara de Ángel and Camila, and *Jane Eyre* by Charlotte Brontë, because his mother had liked it. But when he realized that Nanda hadn't even touched them, he stopped bringing her things to read.

❧

Enea's serenity did not escape his mother, but instead of calming her anxieties, it increased them. Matilde was well aware that any violent emotional explosion burns out in a short time, reaching the magnitude it is destined to produce within the arc of its duration. It then gives way to a period of calm, more or less long, more or less steady, and starts to build up again only after a crisis, preparing to explode all over again. The pattern was as valid for heart attacks and asthma as it was for attacks of depression or homicidal rage. When he struck, the murderer was at the peak of the crisis, and afterward remained inert for several months. Then he came back to strike again. Even if Matilde did not formulate the thought exactly in these terms, the concept nested in her mind.

Enea did not go out in the evening any more, and in fact, he withdrew to the quarters above the lemon-tree room early. The noises that the ceiling echoed back to her were reassuring. He had started to walk around in his slippers again and stayed for hours at the table in his study or the bench in the workshop. (Matilde was able to perceive exactly where her son was sitting from the different creaking sounds made by the chairs and from the point at which they reached her.) When he came downstairs to go to the kitchen or the bathroom, he tried not to make any noise. Even his breathing seemed calmer, no longer broken by the difficulties of late.

❧

"You'll see, you'll see," Enea was saying to Nanda, "you're well now, and everything will be all right. You're gorgeous."

"Stop it!" she repeated. "Can't you see I'm bloated?"

"You don't want to admit it, but you've put on some weight," laughed Enea. "Now you'll find a job, and you'll leave everything bad behind you."

When she was still living with her family and had not started taking drugs, Nanda had gone to a professional secretarial school. Enea thought about asking Andreino Colamele to hire her, at least to work half-days.

For a few months, he had not even been forced to look up George Lockridge, and he hoped he never would have to again. He did not even know if he had returned from his vacation. It was Lockridge who came looking for him. He appeared at the front door of his house one evening right after dinner. Seeing the windows open and the lights on, he rang the doorbell and loudly called out the names of Matilde and Enea. Matilde was forced to invite him inside but remained stiff and unsmiling, staring at the young man that the Englishman dragged along behind him, who was introduced to her simply by his first name.

"This is Luca," said Lockridge, and Matilde replied, "Pleased to meet you," and that was all.

Luca could have been about twenty years old. He wore his curly hair hanging loose to his shoulders and was tightlipped, as if it took him too much effort to speak. Matilde could have sworn he had mascara on his eyelashes. As if that were not enough, he was wearing a pink silk outfit with tight pants and shirt.

George accepted the coffee that Matilde offered, but, he said, none for Luca, he couldn't drink it in the evening. "If he does, he can't sleep and keeps me awake all night," he added, his same old look turning allusive. Matilde caught a hint of something obscene in the Englishman's voice. He seemed very different from the way she had seen him at the Impruneta house. Less meek. Almost immodest.

George told Luca (as if he cared), about his friendship with Nanni and Matilde, and digressed into the artistic sensibilities that had been lost. But, he concluded, "Not Enea. Enea hasn't lost them—his sensibilities. He would be a great sculptor if he didn't limit himself to carving wood. You still carve wood, don't you, Enea?"

Enea muttered yes, with little conviction.

"I would love it if you would do a bust of Luca. Don't you think something about him recalls the angels by Melozzo da Forlì?" He furtively ran his hand down the nape of the young man's neck, changing the subject. "Why don't you show us some of your work?"

Enea tried to put him off, but when he noticed the look on his mother's face as she scrutinized the Englishman, he made up his mind to take him up to the workshop.

Matilde was happy to be free of their presence. In fact, she made it clear right away that she was going to bed so they would not pass by that way again before they left. However, she kept straining to hear, as if their dragging footsteps and the muffled voices might reveal the real purpose of George's visit. She was sure that if the Englishman had turned up there that way he had to have something in mind, but she could not imagine what. That he had reappeared in their lives that way unsettled her.

Upstairs, George was quite simply blackmailing

98

Enea, neither more nor less, even though his words were not explicit.

"What's going on? Do people just drop out of sight from their friends' lives like that?" he was saying. "I wouldn't like to think that of you especially, Enea. If you prove me wrong I'll be happy, but I'm starting to get a bad suspicion. Do you belong to the hordes, unfortunately not dwindling, who are there when they want something, and just vanish when they don't need anything anymore?"

George was sitting on the edge of the table and kept moving books and papers around distractedly. Luca had gone over to lean against the wall, with his arms crossed over his chest, and was staring at Enea with a look of curiosity that he didn't even try to hide.

"This time I'm the one who needs help," continued George. "If I've exposed myself with you up to now, I only did it out of the friendship that bound me to Nanni, and you know it. Now I'm forced to do it out of the friendship that binds me to myself."

"I can't," Enea replied. "Mama would notice, sooner or later. They're all things that we're fond of . . ."

"Come on, come on," the Englishman interrupted him. "Isn't the theory of affective detachment from objects yours? Weren't you the one who said that if objects have conveyed their beauty to you there is no longer any need to possess them, since they have already performed their mission? And speaking of beauty, when I was at the Impruneta house I saw that little landscape painting by Abbati again. You know, that one with the boat on the Arno. Certainly it doesn't mean that much to you. It has such a mannered style, tied to a way of painting that lacks any currency now. It would be easy for me to give it up . . ." Lockridge never used the word sell. "I know a collector that it might interest."

"I can't be away from Florence, these days. Not even to run up to the Impruneta house. I have an obligation that takes up all of my time."

"There's no hurry," the Englishman interrupted him again. "There's no hurry at all. You just need to get it to me early next week."

✦

The next morning when Enea got up, Matilde had already been up for more than two hours. She followed his movements, in and out of his bedroom and in and out of the bathroom, until she knew from a long silence that he was giving himself his insulin shot. She ordered Saveria to put the pot of coffee and pitcher of milk on the table. As soon as her son sat down she started to subject him to a cautious questioning. She began with a preamble on how strange the Englishman's sudden reappearance was, two times no less in such a short space of time, after so many years of not seeing him.

"I can't come up with an answer," she said. "But I feel like that man has something in mind. What do you think he might want?"

"Maybe old age is making him nostalgic," answered Enea vaguely. "Or perhaps he simply wanted to show off the homes he is able to frequent to his young friend."

"I don't believe it could be that simple," said Matilde. "And you can't believe it either."

Enea was becoming irritated. "Well, why should I know anything about George's intentions? You know him better than I, seeing as how he was your friend and

100

Papa's. If anything, you should explain to me why he came to visit us two times for no apparent reason."

Matilde stiffened, "Enea, there's no need to raise your voice."

"I'm not raising my voice at all!" he shouted. "You, though, seeing as how you're so good at pretending to ask other people for opinions, give me your opinion. Tell me if these were the friends you were so proud of when you pretended to entertain a cultural salon."

He continued to stitch strange bits of conversation together, mixed with expressions of hate for that home, and Matilde could not understand the reason for so much anger. Again, she was afraid.

In the end, Enea yelled some other incoherent remarks and threw the napkin down on the table. He ran out without putting anything else on, going out into the rain that had been pouring down since early morning.

At that point, Matilde forgot about the argument and started worrying about her son's health. He had not even touched his milk and was risking another attack of hypoglycemia.

᠅

"But what are you doing going around in this weather without an umbrella?"

Enea had just gotten off the bus in Piazza San Marco, pushed along by the people pressing up against his back. The smell of wet clothes stung his nose, and the rain ran down his neck, clear under his shirt. Beside him was Aldo Mazzacane, smiling timidly as he offered him his own umbrella. "My car is just a short way from here. If you want, I'll give you a ride."

Enea gave a sign of annoyance. That man was starting to get on his nerves with his honey-coated voice and his little smiles of embarrassment. He was about to turn down the offer, but he was late, very late. Anyway, sooner or later that man would find a way to talk to him. He got into the gray car reluctantly, already feeling the sense of foreboding that Mazzacane would say something irritating too.

And so it was.

"I hope that everything is still going well with Nanda," he said meekly, as soon as he turned on the car.

"It couldn't go any better," replied Enea, realizing that his voice was still shaking nervously from the argument with his mother. "As soon as I have time I'll look for a job for her and everything will be all right."

As if Enea had not said anything, Aldo Mazzacane started a strange conversation that broke all of the rules he had always observed.

"Maybe it would be better if I didn't say anything," he said, "but for me it is almost a matter of conscience. If I were you, I wouldn't completely believe in Nanda's intentions. She has already tried to get off drugs in the past. Afterwards it's worse."

"Don't worry. It's different this time. Nanda is determined to put an end to this ugly story. If anything, I'm the one at fault. I still haven't found her a job."

Aldo Mazzacane kept shaking his head, as if he were truly sorry to have to say the things he was saying. "I hope I'm wrong, but in your place, I would keep a closer eye on her. How can anyone know what she's up to when she's alone? Believe me, when they're in that state, they're incorrigible liars. I wouldn't be surprised if while we're here talking, my wife was already going around searching desperately high and low."

Enea lost his head and started yelling like a madman. "It's not surprising Nanda's had all the problems she's had, with people like you around her!" He had turned purple and kept moving his head. "It's easy to deny trust when someone makes a mistake. It's harder to ask oneself which breakdowns are provoked. I'll tell Nanda to be very careful not to be around her so-called relatives from now on if this is their attitude!"

Aldo Mazzacane, who had been motivated by sincere intentions, was frightened by Enea's distorted appearance. It was as if he had become inflated with anger, enough so that he completely filled up the narrow space on his side of the car, with his head up against the low roof, his arms crossed, his legs bent at a right angle.

All of a sudden, Enea turned his big head toward him, and his body seemed to deflate instantaneously. "It would be better if you let me out," he muttered, his voice almost back to normal. "I'll make it there faster on foot."

࿓ࣿ

While Enea was getting out of Aldo Mazzacane's car, Matilde was about to take the keys from the kitchen cabinet. At the memory of the drawing she had found the last time she was up in his study, she had strongly resisted making that decision. Yet the resolution that she could not shrink from any kind of suffering if she really wanted to understand what was happening to her son had given her courage. She could not say precisely how and why, but George Lockridge's visit had to play some part in the madness that hung in the air lately in San Domenico. Otherwise, she couldn't explain Enea's reaction that morning.

Matilde was hoping to find some signs, some sort of proof that might help her to understand. But when she put her hand out to take the keys, she heard the phone ring. She kept the ringer on low because the only sounds in the house were her own footsteps and Saveria's. Any sounds from the outside were blocked out by the deep garden and the tall boxwood hedge, and so she did not need the telephone to ring loudly. Yet, when the soft sound reached her she was startled, as if it were a scream. She stood still for a long while, feeling as if she were about to be sick. As she went all the way into the living room she made an effort to walk standing up straight and picked up the phone almost with repulsion. No matter who it was, she did not feel like talking to anybody.

It was her brother-in-law, Dono, who asked her how she was and why on earth she had taken so long to answer. Matilde did not give any explanation, and, in fact, she asked, "And what about you? Why in the world are you phoning at this hour?"

"Any time at all is good if I can have news about my brother's family. All the more so since my nephew never comes to see me. Speaking of my nephew, didn't Enea tell you it's been two months since he was supposed to come to Morigi's office to have blood drawn for some tests? No one has seen him at all here at the hospital. Glucose levels should be checked often. You know that too. If someone's child doesn't have enough sense to take care of himself, the mother is the one who has to see to it."

Dono was the head physician of gynecology at the Santo Giovanni Hospital, the same one in which Matilde's husband had started his career and where he had been struck dead by a heart attack while operating on a patient. Matilde was convinced that her brother-in-law was hired at Santo Giovanni and subsequently acquired the position of head physician in part due to the prestige his brother had enjoyed and also to his death.

"You must have some other reason for phoning," she said. "You can't expect me to believe that you called at this hour just to ask me about Enea. Shouldn't you be on the ward or in the operating room?"

"It was precisely while we were making rounds that Morigi complained about Enea. So I thought it was a good idea to call you. Tell your son that Morigi is expecting him tomorrow morning at eight. He's not to miss the appointment."

Matilde thanked him, still not very convinced, and promised that she would give him the message. When she hung up she stood there with her hand wrapped tightly around the receiver, reluctant to let it go, as if breaking contact with the black Bakelite could prevent her from continuing to reason things through clearly. She ended up not going upstairs to the quarters above the lemon-tree room. Soon afterward, Saveria returned home with the groceries, and Matilde would never have let the housekeeper find her in her son's study when he was not there.

13

Toward the end of autumn, the weather turned beautiful again. Enea went to have blood drawn for his tests and told his mother about the results, which, though they were not the best possible, were not the worst either. At the same time, two apparently unrelated episodes occurred that would have a great impact on the lives of mother and son.

Enea still had not done anything concrete to find a job for Nanda except for asking half-heartedly here and there if someone might need a secretary. He had not spoken about the young woman to Andreino Colamele because something had always held him back at the last moment. Enea was paralyzed by a sort of modesty that prevented him from mixing his personal affairs with everything else. Asking the notary would be his last resort. For now there was no need to hurry.

Nanda had recovered, and he intended to discuss the more involved decisions with her. For some time he had been mulling over an idea, and the more he thought about it, the more it seemed right. Nanda had to go to some school that would refine her and provide a stronger education than what she had had as a business secretary without even a diploma. In the meantime, he would look for a more spacious and less expensive apartment that he could furnish with pieces of furniture that had been shut up in the garage at the Impruneta house for years. They had inherited the furniture ages ago, and though it was not valuable, at least it represented a solid start for setting up house.

One day while he was telling Nanda about his plans, she suddenly got out of her chair and started to wander around the room. She went into the kitchenette, heated up some milk, and lit the gas burner under the coffee pot. All the while, she was scratching her entire body, as she often did. Enea was used to it by now and did not make that much out of it this time either.

"At least make an effort to give your opinion," he said. "It concerns your life, and you have to be the one to decide."

Enea lifted up his big leather bag from the floor and put it on the table. He pulled out the catalogue for a language school. "Look how interesting this is. The courses include trips abroad too. Wouldn't you like to travel? I traveled very little, and now I regret it. We could go together."

Nanda took the catalogue and leafed through it distractedly. "It's boiling. Would you pour the milk and coffee into a cup for me?" When he brought her what she had asked for, she added, "I'm out of cigarettes."

"That's why you're edgy," said Enea. "I'll dash out to buy some."

He ran all the way to the tobacco shop, which was more than three hundred yards away, and came back anxious to discuss his plan. He gave her the cigarettes and began talking about the language school again.

"Listen to me," Nanda interrupted him almost immediately. "Today is really not the day for this. I'm going out of my mind and I don't want to hear any talk about schools. Why don't you go out for a walk, and then come back this evening?"

Enea understood that it was better to postpone it. He put the catalogue back with the other papers, picked up the bag, and went out, promising that he would come back and see her around dinner time. Since he had some extra time on his hands, he decided to go all the way to the bookseller behind the courthouse. He had asked the bookseller to look for the first edition of *Correspondencia de Fabrique Mendes* by Queirós for him and had never found a moment to see how the search had gone.

The bookseller had acquired the volume for him, rebound in leather by the prior owner and still in excellent condition. The price he was asking for it was within reason. Enea opened his bag, where he had put the money from the paycheck that he had just cashed, and did not find the money. He turned the bag upside down, scattering papers and books, but not even a single bill. He decided he must have pulled the money out at Nanda's house when he had shown her the catalogue and then forgotten it on the table.

"I'm sorry, but I left my money somewhere," he stammered, his face red with agitation. "I'll return later to pick up the book."

"You must be joking!" exclaimed the bookseller, putting the volume into the open bag. "You can come back later to pay for it."

Enea set out toward via de' Renai. He went at a brisk pace, as he usually did, but the bag weighed him down so heavily on one side it made him lopsided. When he arrived, Nanda was not there. He prepared to wait, regretting for the first time that he had not accepted the keys the young woman had offered him when she had first moved into the apartment.

Not wanting to just stand there on the sidewalk, Enea started to walk around the block, taking long, fast steps and counting them one by one to make the time pass by. When it became dark he finally resigned himself to the idea that Nanda was not going to arrive. He was not worried, and did not think anything bad about it either. He was convinced that since Nanda had been in such a bad mood when he left, she must have gone out to get a little air somewhere and had met someone.

He was about to give up when he saw her appear suddenly from a side street, herded along in a group of young people. Her head was lolling around in every direction, in that manner that Enea had learned to recognize so well. He drew back into the entryway nearby and waited until Nanda had gone in with the others. Then he ran away.

꧁ꥇ

". . . a pair of surgical gloves, found at the site of the last double homicide. There is no doubt that they belong to the killer. It could be a message left for the investigators."

Matilde went back into the sitting room as the television was broadcasting the last part of the news. As always, the information was doled out in bits and pieces. She was not surprised when the anchor only added that the police and the district attorney's office had not made any statements.

That night she tossed and turned in bed. During the brief intervals when she managed to fall asleep, she had the recurring nightmare that she was in a dark alley with someone pushing her from behind.

"Go get the newspaper right away," she said to Saveria the next morning. As soon as the woman returned, she laid it out on the dining room table. The gloves had been found along with the dead bodies of the two Germans, but the investigators had decided to keep the piece of news undisclosed until that moment. There were two interpretations. Having discovered that he had killed two men and was left without a woman's dead body to violate, the killer might have thrown away the gloves in a gesture of frustration, not realizing what he was doing. Or else he might have wanted to throw out a challenge to the people who were hunting him down. This detail, in any case, increased the suspicions that he might be a doctor. According to the newspaper, the fact that gloves had been found for the first time did not mean the killer had not used them before. Indeed, it was likely that he always protected his hands, both so he would not leave any fingerprints and so he would not get blood all over his hands. In the same newspaper, one article maintained the gloves were new, if not even still sealed up in their plastic bag inside the box in which they were sold. Another one claimed they had been found turned inside out, as if the man had torn them off in a hurry. Matilde was familiar with that type of glove. They were already on the market when Nanni was still alive and were widely used in all of the hospitals.

When Professor Dono Monterispoli was informed that his sister-in-law wished to see him, his first reaction was to become alarmed. She had never come to see him at Santo Giovanni Hospital, and now all of a sudden she was there, without even calling to let him know in advance. Matilde was not the type to impose on people, and he actually resented her a little because of that excessive reserve.

When his brother died, Dono Monterispoli had expected his sister-in-law to depend on him for financial as well as medical advice, but she had never asked for anything. Even during the time when Dono had figured she might be in menopause, and had offered to examine her himself, alluding to "chemical aids" and the difficulty of facing certain moments alone. Matilde had seemed as if she did not understand. She had looked at him with her blue eyes, slightly dulled by age, and had told him that she was very grateful to him but did not think she needed any treatment.

During the first months he knew her Dono had thought of Matilde as the kind of young woman that he would have wanted too, reaching the point of envying his brother with a resentment that bordered on hostility. Yet as the years passed he had ended up viewing her as merely a practical woman, if somewhat cold, capable of keeping the family estate intact.

When he entered his office, he found her standing in front of the glass door of the medical cabinet with her glasses on, bending over to examine what was inside, and he thought he understood. Dono Monterispoli, who as Matilde suspected was not exactly a genius, prided himself on being a subtle psychologist, of the female mind most of all. He immediately decided that his sister-in-law had come to have him give her an exam, but the sight of his medical instruments had frightened her.

Matilde did not notice Dono right away. When he greeted her, taking her by the arm, she gave a start, as if she had been surprised in the act of stealing something. She put her glasses back in their case and then into her small purse, and felt she had to give an explanation.

"I thought that type of glove wasn't used anymore," she murmured, pointing her hand toward the glass case.

"They are, they are," replied Dono. "I assure you, you can't feel them."

He had her sit down in front of his white enameled desk, and he went to get settled in the chair on the other side, determined to let her take the initiative in the conversation. Seeing as how she accepted the idea of having an exam after so many years, it was better to spare her the embarrassment of pointed questions. He leaned comfortably back in his chair, looking her in the face, aware of the handsome figure he cut in the elegant white doctor's coat, gold-rimmed glasses, his slender face crowned with a mass of gray hair.

"I came about Enea," said Matilde after a moment. "I'm worried." She hesitated, and Dono thought the hesitation confirmed his supposition that she was not there about her son, but for herself. Without further comment, he let her know that in this case he would have her speak with Enea's attending physician. He called the nurse to have her ask Doctor Morigi to come up to his office in half an hour.

He gave himself a half hour because he thought it would take that long to convince his sister-in-law to talk about her own health concerns and then let herself be examined. Since half an hour would pass by quickly, and Matilde was skirting the issue, he decided to speed things up.

"I saw you looking suspiciously at my instruments before," he said with a smile, "but you don't have anything to worry about. Women really ought to have a brief check-up at least a couple of times a year, especially at a certain age. You won't even notice a thing." He broke out in a laugh. "I'm famous in the city for my light touch and slender hands." He put his hands out so she could look at them, turning them on one side and then the other.

Matilde stared at him in silence, beginning to grasp the misunderstanding, and replied that perhaps he was right, sooner or later she would make up her mind to have a doctor's exam. She added, "But actually, when was Enea here at your office?"

"So much time has gone by that I don't even remember his face anymore."

"What! Didn't he come for his tests?" insisted Matilde. "How could it be possible he didn't come by your office to say hello?"

"He went straight down to the lab. Then he found out the results from Morigi."

"He didn't pass by here?"

Dono Monterispoli shook his head with resignation. If it made his sister-in-law happy to pretend she had come about her son, then it was worth going along with her. He concentrated so he could remember when he had seen his nephew the last time. As usual, he ran his open fingers through his hair as if by habit, yet in reality, he was fluffing up his hair.

"Do you know you're right?" he said. "He came by my office too, before going down to Morigi's. It must have been about eight o'clock. I found him standing exactly where you were a little while ago, in front of the glass case. Ultimately I'll have to move it somewhere else, or put up some curtains. Everyone who comes in here seems terrorized by my instruments."

Matilde leaned forward in her chair. "How did he look to you?" she asked.

"Like he usually does. Distracted, and in a hurry to leave. But also a little too heavy. After forty, every extra pound takes one year off your life."

Matilde took it as an accusation and hastened to justify herself.

"When he eats at home, I assure you he keeps perfectly in line. Some soup, a small slice of steamed or boiled meat, a bit of salad and a piece of fruit. How can I control him when he's out?"

"He should be more careful," he said judgmentally. "Diabetes cannot be taken lightly. It's a disease that, if treated, doesn't give any cause for worry. But if it's neglected, it can hold some ugly surprises in store."

Contrary to all of Dono Monterispoli's predictions, as it ended up they continued talking about diabetes until Morigi arrived. According to Dono, it was normal that Enea would be very thirsty and make constant trips to the bathroom, but only if it was related to the symptoms of his illness. In any case, these things were still warning signs. His attacks of near delirium were also part of the clinical picture. How strange though, that he would always be so active and never become sleepy.

The half an hour went by without Dono noticing. Morigi arrived, a young, lanky man with his smock hanging from his body like a scarecrow's coat of rags. He just confirmed what the professor had already said.

❧

"Mama, I have some bad news," said Enea, who was waiting for her in front of the gate to their home.

When Matilde returned from the hospital, it was still before noon. She did not have time to be surprised that Enea was already there because he went on to say "Angiolina phoned. There's been a robbery up at the Impruneta house. We have to go because the carabinieri are waiting for us to give a statement."

Matilde did not lose any time in chatter. As soon as her son had brought the car out of the garage they left. They hardly spoke during the ride. Enea drove carefully, his eyes glued to the traffic, his back straight and arms taut.

After they had passed the crossroads before Pozzolàtico Matilde finally murmured, "This has never happened to me in my entire lifetime." She paused, then added, "Perhaps it had to happen sooner or later."

"Angiolina was worried because she couldn't reach you at home," said Enea. "She didn't want you to find out from Saveria, so she called me at the office. She says her husband is all worked up because he's convinced that we'll accuse him of negligence."

When they were at Piazza Buondelmonti and passed in front of the basilica of Santa Maria dell'Impruneta, Matilde quickly made the sign of the cross. "We shall see," she softly said.

They found the estate manager's entire family gathered in the open space in front of the villa, including his little granddaughter, and also two farmers. The police had already investigated the premises, Angiolina said, and now they were waiting for Signora Matilde and Signor Enea in order to find out what was stolen.

"They asked us if we have seen any new faces around lately," she added, staring at Enea as if to throw his constant comings and goings in his face. "But we haven't seen anyone."

The mother and son made the rounds of all the rooms, starting with the spacious dining room with the frescoed ceiling. The cabinet doors were wide open and the drawers were pulled out, a couple of them lying overturned on the floor. Not even a single teaspoon was left of the silverware. The thieves had made away with the Queen Anne salt shakers and candelabras, the San Marco silver place settings, the serving trays, the desert trays, the sugar bowls. A portable television, an old camera, and embroidered table linens had disappeared. Also missing were the few things that Matilde kept in the jewelry box on top of the chest of drawers in her bedroom—some gold chains with medals, a string of cultured pearls, a cameo, and a necklace made of Neapolitan coral.

They had come in through the French door in the kitchen. To reach the wing where the bedrooms were the robbers had to pass through the gallery of paintings, but the pictures were all still in their places. They had ignored the veranda, and the glass display cases containing antique musical instruments had not been tampered with. In Enea's bedroom, on the other hand, the bonheur du jour, a piece of furniture made out of thuja wood, had been smashed to bits, its porcelain plates scattered in pieces on the floor and the small columns broken in two.

Matilde and Enea decided to walk to the police station, though Angiolina and her husband had offered to take them in their car. "If Signor Enea doesn't feel like driving," the estate manager's wife said, "we'll give you a ride." Angiolina was a woman whom hard work had not bent. Lean as an anchovy, she always stood up straight. When she spoke with someone she looked the person right in the eye. Her fifty years of life had left no sign on her smooth skin and black hair, but she did not boast about it. She said that once the years are behind you, there's no denying them.

Matilde replied that she felt the need to walk, and she cut across the forest of Turkey oaks. She had her city shoes on, and the heels sank into the damp leaves. She could hear Enea's weary steps behind her, a sort of thud muffled by the dampness stagnating beneath the layer of leaves, and she regretted having dragged her son along with her.

"Do you want us to go back to get the car?" she asked, stopping.

Enea shook his head.

When they arrived at the police station, they were chilled and tired, and found the chief almost in tears on top of it.

"Around these parts, some things have never happened. It's the first time in twenty years, and you know it, Signora Monterispoli," said the man. "I'm sure it was outsiders. They must not have been professionals. It's clear from the way they forced the kitchen door. Besides that, they only took the most obvious things. They didn't touch the really valuable pieces. Without a doubt it's some gang of drug addicts that came up from the city."

Matilde was on the verge of telling him that the pieces of silver they stole were valuable too, and not only because of how much it all weighed.

The chief had them promise they would have the gratings on the doors and windows fixed. While Matilde spelled out the extent of the robbery, he carefully wrote down every detail of the stolen items. "You'll see. Sooner or later we'll find your things," he assured her. But he did not seem very convinced.

Matilde almost had to console him. The same thing happened with the estate manager when they returned to the villa, even though a deep sadness weighed upon her. Even more than the loss of the things that had been with her throughout her entire life, she was upset by having found her house violated that way. It was the second time it had happened, first at San Domenico with the police, and now at the Impruneta house. She had the feeling all over again that the house would no longer be the same after those strangers had roamed through the rooms, pillaging everything they could.

The estate manager insisted that she and Enea eat at their house. They sat down at the table in the old, updated farm house, located a few hundred yards beyond the villa's garden. While Angiolina put the roast rabbit on the table, along with potatoes filling the air with the aroma of sage, Matilde questioned Cosimo, their youngest child, a dark-haired boy around seventeen years old. He was strong as a young bull, and besides helping his father with the estate, he took evening classes in accounting, with excellent results it seemed.

"Did you notice anything out of the ordinary in the last few days, Cosimo?" asked Matilde, barely touching the food that was in front of her. "Someone who was wandering around, who you had never seen before?"

"If I had noticed something, I would already have spoken about it with my father and the police chief," answered Cosimo.

"Maybe you invited someone yourself," insisted Matilde. "People easily strike up rash friendships at your age."

Cosimo threw his head up and stared at her spitefully. "No, ma'am. I didn't invite anyone, and I don't have anything to do with the robbery."

Angiolina intervened, irritated by the tone Matilde was taking. "Everyone should look to their own, with regard to friends. People can be rash at any age."

Matilde asked her to explain, but Angiolina muttered that anyone with good ears understood. Then she became withdrawn in a stony, definitive silence.

While they were returning to Florence, Matilde began complaining to Enea. "Did you see how they got on their high horses, Angiolina and her son?" she shook her head, unable to believe so much arrogance.

"You, on the other hand, would have done better not to insinuate that it could have been Cosimo who brought people into the house."

Matilde became irritated. "It's clear they have a guilty conscience because I didn't insinuate anything at all. I only asked a question. A legitimate one, at that. Someone must have actually been in our house in order to rob it." When her son did not reply, she added, "Did you see they have two color television sets? And the furniture in the living room, did you notice, it's new? Can you tell me where they get all of that money?"

"If you think it might have been them, you've gone crazy," said Enea. "They've worked for our family for four generations, and there has never been anything missing."

"You don't believe that nonsense about the drug addicts too!" shot back Matilde angrily. "When they're at their wit's end, they pull the drug addicts out of thin air. I would like someone to tell me how a gang of drug addicts up from the city would know that we had so much silverware!"

Enea had decided not to say anything else.

14

When Saveria came into the house waving the newspaper in the air and yelling that it talked about her and Signor Enea, Matilde was about to slap her to make her shut up. All of the windows were open, and she had the feeling that Saveria's voice, accustomed to making itself heard in the open spaces of the Basilicata countryside for years and years, blasted like a trumpet.

For some time, Matilde had associated the newspapers with the killer who murdered couples, and the fact that they would talk about her and her son provoked a nervous reaction. She tore the page out of Saveria's hand, nervously hiding it behind her back. "Leave," she said. "Go into the kitchen."

But Saveria, who had not noticed how pale her mistress was, continued, "It's bad for them to write about all of the valuable things in your house. That way, the next time the robbers will know what is better to take."

Then Matilde finally understood that the woman was referring to the robbery at the Impruneta house. She decided to sit down, and leafed through the newspaper until she found the article. The headline talked about the renewed wave of crime that had broken a relatively calm period of inactivity that had been forced on the crime world after the last double homicide.

There was a photograph of the Impruneta villa with descriptions of each item that was stolen and also of the "valuable art treasures" that were saved. It had a few lines about Matilde, the "widow of a doctor once very famous in the city," and said Enea was forty-nine years old, single, lived with his mother, and worked in a notary office.

It took a while for Matilde to recognize her son in the picture of the young man at the end of the article. She wondered where they could have gotten that photograph, which dated back to when Enea entered shooting matches and had been taken when he had won a medal. Just as soon as the recollection materialized in her memory, Matilde was struck with fear. Now those two policemen would see the photograph, and they would remember him and start to be all over him again. She squeezed her hands so hard she crumpled up the newspaper. Saveria stared at her but did not understand.

"Do you need anything?" she asked. "Aren't you feeling well, ma'am?"

Matilde did not answer. She turned around suddenly and went to shut herself in her bedroom.

It was the first time Saveria had seen her mistress in that state. Even though she had every right to behave strangely, what with the robbers in her home and the article in the newspaper, she decided it was better to let Signor Enea know about it.

Enea rushed home in a taxi, leaving behind Andreino Colamele, who was urging him to phone as soon as he arrived to tell him how his mother was doing. He found Matilde stretched out on the bed with all of her clothes on, including her shoes, the small silk quilt wrapped around her stomach.

"Mama, what's wrong?" he asked, sitting down on the edge of the bed. "Aren't you feeling well?"

Matilde looked at him without answering, surprised to see him there.

"What happened, Mama?" Enea pressed her. "Do you want me to call Uncle Dono?"

"I'm absolutely fine. There's no reason to get worried. I must have caught a chill around my stomach, that's all. It must have been that stupid Saveria who called you."

Enea shook his head, not very convinced. His mother had not been the same for a few months. Lately her eyes were lifeless and she had a look of pain on her face that he had never seen before. He felt guilty for not having done anything about it.

"Did you see the newspaper, Enea?"

"There was no way I could have missed it. They couldn't talk about anything else at the office. They just kept laughing about that old photo of me." He said it sadly, and Matilde imagined that beneath the laughter there had been a hint of derision.

"I was touched by it." She reached out her hand and put it lightly over her son's hand, lying aimlessly near her on the covers. When she saw that Enea did not pull away as he usually did, she squeezed his hand. "We were happy back then."

"Happy?"

"I truly think so. We were a family. We had a long life to live in front of us and then . . . your father was alive." Matilde did not have anything in particular in mind to say to her son, but the fact that he was close to her and inclined to talk seemed like such a rare event that it could not be wasted. "We're defenseless now," she continued. "If we make a mistake, no one can tell us that we have made a mistake."

"But we never make mistakes," exclaimed Enea, in an attempt to lighten the tone.

"People often don't notice the errors they commit." Matilde realized she was voicing empty concepts, but she could not resist pushing on to the question that weighed on her mind. "I know you'll laugh, but lately you seem like a little boy to me again. As if you needed protection, but I'm not able to give it to you."

"You always protected me, Mama," said Enea smiling. To overcome the rush of emotion he felt at suddenly seeing her look so old, he added, "Even too much!"

"You laugh, but when a person begins to look at things from a distance, as I look at them, they no longer appear as isolated events. They appear as a unique whole, with a logic and a thread that unite them. You know, when I saw that picture in the newspaper, those summer afternoons at the Impruneta house came back to mind. The times when the heat didn't stop us from running through the garden, vying to see who could gather the most beautiful flowers to put on the table. We always had people over to the house. Your father would laugh with joy when you carved the roast with the skill of a great surgeon, or won a medal in some shooting match."

"I wasn't very happy," said Enea, slowly moving his hand away from his mother's. "All of the people you invited didn't mean anything to me. When Papa put me on display, it made me feel bad."

"You haven't shot a gun again since then, have you?" Matilde finally asked. When her son did not answer, she repeated, "You haven't shot a gun again, have you?" After a moment, "Where did Papa's gun end up?"

"Around here some place," said Enea.

"Didn't you take it to the police?"

"Yes, I took it."

"It ought to be kept oiled if we don't want it to get ruined. Do you at least keep it oiled?" In the end, gathering all the courage she had left, she insisted, "Have you used it again, Enea?"

"When I use it again, it will be to shoot myself in the head."

❧

Enea called the notary to reassure him about his mother's health and to tell him that he was going to stay to keep her company that morning. Instead, he went out to look for Nanda. He could not believe that she might have been the one who planned the robbery at the Impruneta house, and he at least wanted to talk to her. Nanda had gone to the villa just once, when he had taken the copy of the Abbati there, and it seemed as if she had not even looked around. They had stayed just long enough to hang the painting in its place again, so short a time that he had left the car running.

When he had seen her return home with her head drooping from side to side, along with the group of young people, he had sworn to himself that he would not do anything more for her. To reduce herself to that state she had obviously spent the money from his paycheck, even though only he and his carelessness were to blame. If he had not forgotten the money on the table, Nanda would not have found it lying around the house and had the temptation to take it. The idea that the young woman might have stolen it from his bag when he went out to buy her cigarettes had not even dawned on him.

He was so convinced he wanted to break off his relationship with Nanda that he had even faced up to one of the actual problems, like the house on via de' Renai. He did not have any keys to it and Nanda was bringing that riffraff there. Yet, even if he had given notice for the studio, things would not have changed. The owners would have continued to hold him responsible, not only for the rent, but also for everything that happened inside. He really had to talk about it with Nanda and lay down his terms once and for all. He needed to look for some way out. Who knows whether he might not be on the verge of finding it, now that the robbery at the Impruneta house gave him a justification for meeting her.

At that hour Nanda was surely still in bed. He would not mince any words with her. She should not deceive herself, she could not rely on him being there for her any more. She had to stand on her own two feet, and then, who knows, they would see. If she preferred to choose her friends where she was choosing them, she was free to do so, but she should forget about him then, because he was cut from a different cloth. Aldo Mazzacane, poor man, was right. In fact, he would go apologize to him for not listening to his warnings. No, he thought, perhaps he should not say that. Nanda was capable of looking for her ex-husband and making one of her scenes.

When he rang the doorbell at via de' Renai and nobody answered, he thought that Nanda was inside and did not want to let him in. He kept on ringing the bell, and pounded on the door with his fists, yelling for her to hurry it up because he knew she was there anyway. After some time he finally understood the woman was really out. She must have become frightened when she realized what she had done by taking the money from his paycheck, and to avoid his reaction she had gone to find a safe place somewhere.

It was still before noon. Enea continued to wander around the city until late in the afternoon, without noticing the time that passed, or the tiredness that made his legs and feet feel like lead, or his hunger pangs. He crossed the Arno at the Ponte delle Grazie and slipped into the narrow streets behind the church of Santa Croce. He walked straight ahead, his eyes shifting from one side to the other, casting sidelong glances at the groups of young people planted on the corners, ignoring the people who ran into him or insulted him about the way he poked along.

On via della Vigna Vecchia, he ran into one of Colamele's clients, who was in litigation with the other heirs over a house in Peretola that had not yet been divided up. A successful antique dealer, the man was rich enough not to need the portion of the building he would get once the matter was resolved. He planted himself in front of Enea and started enumerating nefarious things about all of his cousins. While he spoke, he pulled at Enea's sleeve every time he seemed distracted. Enea finally jerked away and walked off, leaving him dumbfounded and determined to go to the notary's office and denounce his assistant's behavior.

Enea kept on walking, looking closely in all the nooks and crannies where he thought he might find Nanda. When he realized he was on via Porta Rossa, just a step away from Colamele's office, he pushed on by Palazzo Davanzati, toward via Tornabuoni.

He had often been in those streets to look for pushers, and it was the time of day when they would be making their first appearance. He would have tracked down at least one of them somewhere who would be able to give him some news about Nanda. Instead, he happened to run into Nicolò D'Americo, one of his old classmates from high school and the owner of a real estate agency. Nicolò told him he had some good news. If he was still interested in finding an apartment, he had a once-in-a-lifetime deal right in his hands: a four-room apartment with a terrace, right behind via Lungarno Torrigiani. Enea shook his head, continuing to look around. Nicolò was surprised at first, then he suddenly remembered having read about the robbery at the Impruneta estate. He tried to make up for it, saying that he had heard about the news just by chance, without knowing the particulars, and declared he was sorry it had happened to them of all people. Enea abruptly left him standing there too, without saying goodbye, and Nicolò thought that the robbery must have been more serious than reported.

When it was five o'clock, Enea was walking without even realizing where he was going anymore, or why. His arms dangled at his sides, his head was bowed, and his shoulders sagged with weariness. His long, fast steps had turned into a slow, tired shuffle. He had no intention of stopping though. He found himself alongside the church of Santa Maria Novella, facing the train station, and continued on in that direction just because he had been there recently. The pushers and addicts earned the right to take shelter in the waiting rooms simply by purchasing a ticket for the closest station.

He was drawn to something without realizing it. There were two young men leaning against the wall of a building, and they were staring at him insistently, with their hands in the pockets of their jeans, their fake leather jackets buttoned up to their chins. When their eyes met Enea's, the two men stood up straight, nudged each other, and ran away. If he had not been as tired as he was, he would have recognized them. They were part of the group Nanda had come home with the day the money from his paycheck had disappeared.

He headed toward the station and went in the second-class waiting room without even looking around. He just felt like resting a few minutes. It was Nanda who nodded to him from the bench she was sitting on. Enea went up to her and collapsed heavily beside her, letting his arms drop between his open legs.

"They told me you were on your way here," said Nanda. "Two of my friends. If I had wanted to, I could have left." She looked him up and down. "You're angry with me."

Enea felt so relieved at having found her that he did not think he had to say anything. They would have time to talk. He turned around and did not like what he saw. She was pale, her hair was all messed up, and she was scratching her groin and the insides of her thighs. Her bony knees protruded beneath her wrinkled pants.

"Look at what you've reduced yourself to again," he said, so tenderly it upset Nanda.

"Don't start all over giving me lectures!" exclaimed the young woman, pulling back. "Don't start up again! Understand?!"

Then Enea spotted the pin. Despite the cold, Nanda had on a blue, light knit top with a scooped neckline that left her skinny breastbone bare. To the side, pinned on haphazardly, with the material bunched up below—Matilde's cameo.

"No, not this," murmured Enea, and he reached over to take off the pin.

15

Enea moved around nervously in George Lockridge's narrow shop. He had arrived just a few minutes before, coming straight from Colamele's office, and he already felt caged in. He usually could not stay still, except when he had to immerse himself in reading a book or studying documents.

The shop was narrow, long, and so crammed full of things it gave Enea an oppressive sense of claustrophobia. There were knickknacks and lamps, gilt frames and black frames of every type and size. They were heaped up against the walls and against the pieces of furniture that were stacked on top of each other and precariously balanced, destined to feed the vanity of the people who frequented the store, all of whom were convinced they could discover some work of art to carry away for next to nothing.

Rich professionals and young people without a penny went to George Lockridge's shop, the former searching for some items to buy even under-the-counter, and the latter trying to put together some pieces of furniture to set up house. In the end, they gathered up an old, worm-eaten chest of drawers and a pair of nightstands missing their doors, with which, for want of something better, they hoped to create a *maison de caractère.* They would work for days and days to strip the old surfaces and to line the small stands, transforming them into liquor cabinets. Once chipped vases and enameled basins had been arranged on the shelves next to wooden putti and old brass candelabras, the final result was inevitably funereal.

Over the years, Lockridge had developed the ability to sell his things without even saying which exact period they belonged to or whether they were really what they appeared to be. The client would stop in front of a secretary desk, scrutinize it minutely (the shop's habitués had a certain smattering of knowledge about antiques), and bend over to look at the handles (if they were still there) and the shelves inside. Then they would ask how much the Englishman wanted for that little piece of furniture. George Lockridge answered that if he were not so old and tired he would have restored it himself to take to antique shows, but since by then he was happy just to make it through the day, he would let it go for what it had cost him. He named the price, usually at least ten times higher than the actual value of the piece, and then he did not budge.

That day, as they were getting ready to close for lunch, a thin, elegant man happened to come into the shop, clearly an antique dealer from out of town. He picked up the picture frames one by one and carried them over to the light coming in from the street. He examined them front and back, and then returned them to their place with the fussy air of someone who is forced to do a job beneath his rank.

The Englishman watched him from his corner for about twenty minutes, and then became fed up. "People who are not able to appreciate beautiful things," he said, pretending to talk with Enea, "should not concern themselves with them. If they do, they lose precious time and risk making others lose it too."

He expected the man to have some kind of reaction. Instead, without saying a thing, he chose three frames, not even among the best, and stood right in front of him with his wallet in hand. He paid every last cent without even trying to hint at negotiating the price, but then he wanted to have the last word.

"Beauty is not measured by one yardstick alone," he pronounced. "In my opinion, whatever I can sell above cost is beautiful too."

After the man had disappeared with the frames, Lockridge told Enea that since the morning had gone well, he would treat him to lunch at Gino's, a restaurant with a lot of patrons and a choice of dishes that was slim, but always different and always filling. Since Luca had left him to go away with a young American choreographer, Lockridge seemed even older, and his voice had become weak like a little girl's. He went on complaining about how the more sensitive people are, the more they are destined to suffer. His loneliness had slowly pushed him to become closer to Enea, so much so that he now went to see him even when there were not any paintings to copy or to let go. He sensed that Enea had a problem similar to his, even though he had only managed to pull a few reflections on existence out of him, which, translated into plain words, meant to the Englishman that Enea had also been jilted a few times.

If he happened to talk about Luca, as he did, Lockridge went into the crudest details, at times describing him as an exploiter who had taken away not only all of his money, but also his desire to live. At other times he described him as a thoughtless young man who had let himself become dazzled by the idea of America.

"How is it that you haven't needed any more money for a while?" he asked, when they were seated at the corner table in the restaurant, near the kitchen.

The restaurant was frequented mostly by the shop-keepers in the neighborhood who did not go home for lunch. The menu started unfailingly with a thick chunk of mortadella plunked down on the checkered table-cloth, sitting on a piece of yellow butcher's paper, re-calling bygone days.

"Because I'm alone now," answered Enea, staring at the plate.

The Englishman cut off a piece of mortadella in the shape of a triangle, stuffed it in his mouth and started to chew carefully, afraid that his teeth might move. "It's bad to be alone, believe me. Anything else, but not alone. Rather than that, settle for any compromise. Take any abuse. When people are alone they become pathetic."

Enea raised his eyes to look at him anxiously. "Even when the person you care about forces you to do things you detest and reduces you to a state of powerlessness?"

"Even if they tear out your soul."

❧

Calambrina had been knocking on the kitchen window with her elbow for a few minutes, trying to attract Ma-tilde's attention. Her hands were full of packages and little packets, and her wool cap was about to slip off of her head.

"I've been there outside for half an hour," she shrieked, coming in and giving her a kiss on the cheek. She lost hold of the magazine she was gripping under her arm, bent over to pick it up and then a light blue packet fluttered down. Huffing, she dumped everything onto the table, while Matilde gave her a hand to gather her things back together.

"I just found out this morning about the robbery you had," she exclaimed hurriedly. "We were out of town. I had to make the rounds of all the stores because there wasn't a thing in the house. Why didn't you let me know about it?"

"Because you were out of town," Matilde answered calmly. Calambrina's arrival seemed inopportune, and she had to make an effort to hide her annoyance. She was already imagining the explanations she would want, and how Calambrina would inevitably take the part of the defenseless estate manager and his son Cosimo.

Surprisingly, Calambrina said, "When certain things happen, we have to look to the people who are closest to us. I never really much liked that Angiolina of yours. Hello, Saveria."

Matilde had not even noticed Saveria, who had already returned with a bulky package. When she saw her she had to think hard for a moment before she remembered that she had sent her to the dry cleaner's to pick up Enea's gray suit. Saveria stood there motionless, with her arms stretched out as if she were holding a newborn baby on the day of his baptism, as the long package, wrapped in paper, reached all the way down to her wrists.

"What are you doing? Take it into Signor Enea's bedroom," said Matilde, losing her patience. She immediately understood that Saveria had something unpleasant to tell her. "Come on, come on," she hastened to add. "Go on into the other room." Whatever it might be, she did not want Saveria to talk about it in front of Calambrina.

The woman set the package with the suit down carefully on the marble shelf. She stuck her hand into her pocket. When she pulled her hand back out, she held it open in front of Matilde. "The cleaner says this is yours. They found it in Signor Enea's suit pocket."

Matilde stood motionless, staring at her cameo in Saveria's palm.

"It happens to me too," interjected Calambrina. "I always forget things in my pockets. Luckily there are still some honest people around."

Matilde put her hand out toward Saveria's, without taking her eyes off the woman or picking up the cameo. Saveria held her gaze, dropping the pin in her hand.

That evening Matilde put on a black wool jacket and pinned the cameo on the collar. When Enea came into the dining room she waited for him, standing behind her chair. The entire day, she had put together and taken apart theories about that discovery, but she had not really been convinced by any of them. Enea stopped behind his usual seat and waited for his mother to sit down. She remained standing where she was, staring at him.

"Are we expecting someone?" he asked, noticing she was dressed in black. He saw the pin.

"I think you owe me an explanation." Matilde spoke the sentence that she had prepared, not one syllable more and not one less, and stood there waiting.

Enea met her eyes, had a moment of hesitation, and then replied with all of the dignity he could muster, "Mama, if you want me to lie, I can tell you I found it on the ground up at the Impruneta house when we went there the day of the robbery and stuck it in my pocket without realizing it."

"I don't want you to lie to me. I'm tired of lies. I want you to tell me the truth, whatever it may be."

Enea was about to say something back, but changed his mind. He remained silent for a few seconds, and finally murmured, "If I don't tell you the truth, it's only because you wouldn't understand."

The first time Enea took Nanda to George's house, he was surprised by the young woman's reaction.

"I like it here, I really like it," she cried out loudly, running around the farmyard and then dashing inside to sit down on the floor in front of the lit fireplace.

George lived in one enormous room on the first floor of an old farm house near the Ponte a Ema area, too close to the freeway interchange to be called the country and too far from Florence to be considered the city. Part of the building remained unoccupied, and another section had been turned into a warehouse for a furniture company that had its factory a short distance away. George had obtained his spacious room for a small amount of money in exchange for watching over the place at night.

"Why do you like it so much?" Enea asked Nanda.

"Because it's free here."

George said he would be happy to have them over whenever they felt like it, and so Enea and Nanda began spending Saturday and Sunday afternoons at Ponte a Ema. The Englishman welcomed them warmly and prepared tea for everyone on the wood-burning stove, which was always going. Enea sat on a church pew that was transformed into a couch and watched him in silence most of the time, while he busied himself with the sugar and small pot. Nanda wandered around outside the house if the weather was nice, and if it was bad she crouched in front of the fireplace, her eyes fixed on the flame, lost in thought.

"I'm ashamed," she said to Enea one day, as they were walking around the farmyard right after a storm. "Don't think I'm not ashamed. You can't understand, but it's painful to be like me. Sometimes, I would really like to end it all."

As the weeks went by, the Englishman had become fond of the young woman and showed her kindness too. He yelled at her if she did not agree to eat something, and if he thought it was too cold for what she was wearing, he put one of his old sweaters over her shoulders. "You're thin, you're thin," he grumbled. "Leave the skin and bones to me."

The room was divided into two parts by a large Chinese screen that separated the imposing brass double bed from the rest of the room, and by a low wall that set apart the studio, closer to the window. Old frameless paintings were hanging on the walls, but there was not even one of the landscapes painted by George, who maintained he had sold the last one at least twenty years ago. When he was working on copies of paintings, he moved the screen and hid out of Enea and Nanda's sight.

The young woman did not ask questions and never asked for anything. Out of the blue one day she said something that hung in the air of the large room for several minutes: "We certainly do make a fine trio. An addict, a queer, and a eunuch. And thieves on top of it." She became serious, and added, "At least you two are old." Then she fell asleep on George's bed, all curled up.

The Englishman put the small enameled iron mug, filled to the brim with tea, into Enea's hand, and sat down next to him on the church bench. "You know it can't last, don't you?" he said softly. "She is our alibi, our excuse to go on living. Sooner or later she'll leave us, and we won't have an excuse anymore."

∾✈

At home, Matilde was waiting for her son, who still had not come home. She stayed up until one o'clock, and then went to bed. She took a book from the night-stand, which she had started over a month before and still had not been able to get beyond page fifty, opened it, and stared at the lines.

An unusually strong wind rattled the shutters, shaking the branches of the trees, and Matilde thought about how the garden would be full of leaves the next day. She was surprised at that thought.

∾✈

Enea was shoved with his face up against the wall, his hands open flat on the rough surface, his arms raised. He felt his legs being spread apart from behind while the two police officers quickly patted him down, running their hands over his pockets, the insides of his legs, around his ankles. He felt stunned, but was not afraid. He had gone clear out to that neighborhood beyond San Frediano to get a packet for Nanda. Shortly after he and the pusher had exchanged the money and dope, bright headlights had come on in the dark lane, catching his entire body and lighting up every corner clear to the other end where a van was parked across the street, blocking the exit.

"Don't move," whispered the small, thin pusher,

standing beside Enea with his face up against the wall and his arms raised too. "These guys aren't from Narcotics. I'll handle it. You just stay quiet."

Enea let the policemen turn him around to face them, and then push him toward the van blocking the street. At that point the pusher started to yell, shoving his hands in his pockets and turning the lining inside out: "I'm clean! You caught me clean!"

"Then explain where you got all the money you had on you," said one of the officers, giving him a shove.

"I got myself a sugar daddy. There's no law to stop someone from paying me if he likes me."

Enea looked around, turning his head in every direction, trying to see what was happening in the dark street. He felt the pusher's hand slip into his right pocket as they were being pushed into the van.

"Just think about keeping quiet," the man told him again, pulling his hand out. "Now you're clean too."

"Thanks," mumbled Enea.

The van was loaded with people rounded up from the streets in the neighborhood. It seemed as if everyone knew each other.

"We're spending another night in the police station, and what does it really matter," said a distinguished man, seated in a corner.

"Pretty-eyes," the pusher said to him, "if you noticed anything strange while lurking among the bushes as you exercised your functions as a Peeping Tom, please tell our honorable police officers about it. Then they'll finally nab that fucking Monster and we'll start having some room to breathe again."

Enea had landed between an old man who smelled of wine and a prostitute who hugged her fur jacket tightly around her.

"My God, you're so big," said the woman to Enea, who was keeping his legs together and his arms crossed over his chest so he would take up less space. "I bet not even the Monster is as big as you."

Enea's eyes sought out the pusher, looking at him questioningly, and the pusher replied that snow had fallen on the earth and soon the flowers would bloom.

"Shut up," said one of the two policemen, as he hoisted himself into the van too. "Shut up, and don't kick up the usual ruckus."

"Look," the distinguished gentleman asked, "do you really think one of us may be able to tell you something useful? If we actually knew something, we would run straight in to tell you. Then you'd leave us in peace."

"You be quiet too, Pretty-eyes," said the same officer as before.

Even in that moment, Enea thought about Nanda, who was waiting for him on via de' Renai, and was happy he had insisted on going himself to pick up the packet. The wind seeped inside the van, and everyone was huddled over, stomping their feet on the floor. He was not afraid of any possible legal consequences. He knew that at the very most they would detain him at police headquarters until the next morning, and then they would release him. If they had found the packet on him, it would have been worse. Since he did not have any signs of needle marks on his arms, he would not have been able to maintain that the heroin was for his own personal use. Instead, he was worried about Nanda. When he had left her over an hour earlier, she was already restless. Now, failing to see him return, she would hit the streets looking for him. She risked being slammed into a van too. That night, the city seemed under siege.

They were unloaded in front of a main entrance and pushed inside a large, crowded room. A few people were sitting on the floor with their heads down between their arms. A police officer would come in every five minutes and signal to the person who was supposed to be interrogated, taking him away. At that rate, Enea estimated, it would take at least three hours before it would be his turn. Instead, he was called almost immediately. The officer saw him towering above the others and said to follow him.

Beyond the door of the large room there was a small office with pea green walls, a desk, and a man of about fifty seated on the other side of it. Beside him, sitting behind a smaller desk, a young man pounded on the keys of a typewriter. The older man looked at Enea.

"Why did you bring this one in?"

"Because he was in the neighborhood."

"Do you have a record?" the man asked Enea.

"If you mean a criminal record, no. I have a clean record."

"Did you find anything on him?" This time the man addressed the police officer.

"No, sir."

"Check his documents, then let him go."

❧❧

Matilde was sitting in bed with the lamp on the night-stand turned on. It was almost three o'clock, and Enea still had not come home. She again picked up the book that she had left open, put it in front of her eyes, looked at it for a short while, and put it down again. She checked the alarm clock for the umpteenth time. The wind made the shutters shake, and the tree branches whipped against the side of the house. Matilde started to wonder if, by chance, Enea might have come in, and she had not heard him because of all that noise.

She strained her ears to see if she could hear any movement from the quarters over the lemon-tree room or the rest of the house. When the telephone rang she heard it distinctly. She had almost expected the phone or the doorbell to ring. She went to answer it without even slipping on her robe.

"Hello?" she said. She added two words she usually did not say: "Monterispoli residence."

"Is Enea there?" a female voice asked.

It was a strange voice, so weak and broken that it seemed as if it were disguised.

"Hello? Who's speaking?" said Matilde.

"Is Enea there?" repeated the voice, more loudly.

"No, Enea's not here," replied Matilde. "Do you mind telling me who is calling?"

The woman on the other end hung up.

A young man started to shake all of a sudden, clutching his arms around his body, and slid down the wall until he was sitting on the stone floor. Enea looked at him a moment and recognized the onslaught of withdrawal. Soon afterward the vomiting would start, and the room would become uninhabitable. So he went over to the policeman standing in the doorway, with his back turned toward the inside of the room, and said, "That gentleman is ill."

The policeman turned to look at Enea, but did not understand. Enea pointed to the boy on the floor. Everyone had suddenly stopped talking and had turned around toward them. The officer headed over to the young man, grabbed him by the front of his shirt, and

141

made him stand up. "Get yourself on home. Just take off," he said. Then he looked at Enea again. "What are you still doing here? We're done with you. Didn't any-one tell you?"

Enea asked if he could call a cab, and the policeman pointed to a public phone at the end of the hall.

When he arrived at via de' Renai, Enea already knew he would not find Nanda there. He had the cab wait, and since there was no answer when he rang the bell repeatedly, he asked the driver to take him to San Domenico.

16

The two young people are in the backseat of the car. She is eighteen years old, he is twenty-three. They love each other and are about to make love. The girl takes off her blouse and her bra, which are still hanging half-way down her arm. She has thrown her jeans on the front seat, while the boy has draped his over the back of the seat. They are laughing.

The place is called the Boschetta and is near Vic-chio, in Mugello. The field of alfalfa stretching out a short distance away gives off a pungent smell, similar to newly cut hay. The car is on a steep path, surrounded completely by shrubs and underbrush. It seems to dis-appear into the darkness of the new moon. If the car does not move, it is only because the hand brake keeps it firmly parked.

On the right side, there is just enough space for the door to be opened half way. On the left, it is com-pletely blocked by the thick vegetation.

Still, the hulking dark shadow manages to make its way through the branches and reach the window on the right side. He puts the gun barrel up against the closed window and pulls the trigger. The first bullet hits the boy in the ear, the second one in the chest, the third in the diaphragm, the fourth in the chest again.

The boy refuses to die. He curls up on the seat, clasps his knees tightly to his chest, and screams—he screams as blood streams over him.

The man shoots again, trying to follow the boy's wild movements with his aim, and this time he only hits the pants hanging over the back of the front seat. The boy seems to be overcome with convulsions. He gives a long heave of vomit.

When he is certain that he has finished off the boy, the man slightly moves the barrel of the gun and shoots at the girl. Just one shot that after grazing her arm, raised in a futile attempt to defend herself, hits her in the jaw, shattering it.

The man opens the door, getting it stuck in the bushes, and bends over, into the car. The boy's body shudders one last time. The man, who already has the knife unsheathed, brings it down several times, sinking it into the flesh, violently at first, and then more and more weakly, almost as if he were drained by the initial force imparted to the blows, and is now moving on inertia alone, not even able to injure the muscle tissue.

Finally he can grab the girl under her arms to drag her out of the car. She is wearing only bikini underpants, and has clusters of chains around her neck and wrists that tinkle while her body is pulled out of the car in fitful tugs.

The man moves with difficulty in the narrow space between the car and the wall of branches. He continues to drag the girl and uses his shoulders to force his way through the bushes. Walking backward, he reaches the alfalfa field. He lays the lifeless body down, stands up to his full height, lifts his hands into the air with his face turned toward the black sky. Then he bends down again over the motionless body, brandishing the knife.

He lowers his arm, raises it up, lowers it again, all in a single motion. The knife sinks into the girl's head twice, then slips between her skin and panties and tears the light material.

Now the man works with the edge of the blade. He lightly cuts the left breast seven times. He knows the consistency of the skin now, how elastic it is. He moves to the right breast, and with a single circular motion he cuts it clean off. He lays the fetish on the grass next to the body, and begins to mark the outline of the pubis all the way down to the back, drawing a U that makes it possible for him to take out the entire strip with one pull, accompanied by a sharp flick of the wrist.

His hand gropes around in the dark to find the severed breast on the grass. It is the first time that the man has taken possession of a breast. He lets out a long rumbling sound of triumph and goes away, his feet sinking into the alfalfa.

❧❧❧

The night the killer carried out his double murder at the Boschetta, Matilde did not remember there was a new moon. When she went to bed, she had no particular reason to feel uneasy. Enea had not gone out that evening. He had stayed in the quarters above the lemon-tree room, and because of the silence, she imagined that he was reading.

Lately the relations between the two of them had undergone a strange change. Enea had started to give her some explanations, and even though she was not entirely convinced by them, if nothing else, this showed her son had greater respect for her feelings. He had refused to talk any more about the cameo, but the night he had gotten home at nearly four o'clock and had found her still awake with the light on, he had stopped by her room. Without even asking her if she was all right, he had said, "Something happened to me that I would never have thought possible." Since he seemed truly shaken, Matilde had invited him to sit down next to her. Enea had dropped onto the edge of the bed, shaking his head. "I was coming out of the movie theater when I was caught in a police roundup. I was suddenly thrown together with prostitutes, pimps, Peeping Toms, and young boys. Some of them were really young."

Matilde felt her heart skip a beat, but he seemed so upset, so tired, that she suddenly thought there was not any reason to worry. If Enea told her that story, it meant that it was truly a matter of an error on the part of the police. It had surprised him too.

"While we're here in our home, not really living after all, there's a city outside that exists only at night," continued Enea. "You know what struck me the most? That everyone knows each other and seems to be fond of each other. Even the police. There's almost a sort of familiarity between the police officers and those people."

One day he tried to explain to her why for a while he had been going to the country on Saturdays and Sundays, to a friend's house, whose name he did not mention, on the outskirts of Florence. "It's free there," he said. Matilde asked him why in the world he did not go up to the Impruneta house, a place he had always loved. He shook his head. "It's not the same thing. Where I go, there is only one large room with a farmyard out in front." It seemed as if he expected her to understand.

The night the killer struck again, Matilde had seen a fairly enjoyable film on television, and when she turned out the light she fell asleep before she even had time to say a prayer. She must have been calm only on the surface since the mere sound of Enea pushing his chair back on the floor upstairs made her eyes shoot wide open in the dark. She groped around to find the alarm clock on the nightstand and cast a sidelong glance at its glowing hands. It was ten minutes past midnight.

She was surprised that such a short time had passed since she had gone to bed. She felt as if she had slept all she needed to get a full night's rest. She put the alarm clock up to her ear, thinking that it might have stopped, and instead she clearly heard it ticking away. She wondered what had given her such a start, and remembered. Enea had moved.

She held the alarm clock in her hand, craning her head toward the ceiling. Enea had opened the study door and was coming down the stairs, walking as quietly as possible, softly putting one foot down after the other before shifting the weight of his body. He opened the downstairs door too, which rustled imperceptibly, and closed it without making the least bit of noise—Matilde followed his every movement because she knew him so well, and did not need to interpret the creaking or knocking. Enea came down the hallway next to the sitting room in front of his mother's bedroom, the runner barely whispering, and went out of the house. He left by the front door and went down the path, but despite how careful he was, the gravel crunched.

Matilde got out from under the covers, her hand clutched around the dainty collar of her cotton nightgown, and she peeked out between the slats of the shutters. She saw Enea, or rather, Enea's legs, in front of the gate. They were firmly planted, like two large columns, and it seemed to Matilde as if time stood still. In her mind she pleaded with her son to come back inside, to renounce going wherever he may have decided to go. Just when it seemed as if her pleas had been heard and were answered, his legs suddenly moved. The gate moaned open and they disappeared from sight, his feet turned to the right, toward the city.

Matilde went back to bed and sat in the dark, her back against the walnut headboard. She was not praying, but it was as if she were. What was for her an indeterminable space of time went by. When she heard the steps on the path again, the darkness beyond the shutters was fading.

Enea did not go into his bedroom. He went upstairs again and moved around in the two rooms, going back and forth without trying not to make any noise. Something fell loudly on the floor, as if some object, not heavy, but made of metal, had slipped out of his hands.

When her son came downstairs, Matilde was already dressed and the bedroom clock said seven-thirty. At eight o'clock, Enea was in the dining room, ready to leave. He had dark circles under his eyes and the skin on his face sagged. He kept his eyes fixed on his cup of milk. As he opened the front door, he muttered something that could have been a goodbye.

◦◦◦

This time Matilde decided to go up to the quarters above the lemon-tree room. If Enea went out, she would carry out her plan that same evening. In fact, she would do it as soon as Saveria had left, before her son came home for dinner.

The quarters over the lemon-tree room had started to obsess her since Lockridge and his young friend had dropped in. She was sure they were hiding some secret or at least a key to understanding her son's recent behavior. Knowing the rooms so well, she imagined them down to their smallest detail, but as if each detail were deformed by a distorted perspective. In her mind, the table was transformed into the long deck of a ship, seen through binoculars that were slightly out of focus, and the books heaped on the shelves became a long slit that was difficult for Enea to pass through, hemmed in on both sides by masses of printed paper. The rooms were freezing in her imagination, and the dust that gathered everywhere was a sticky substance, repugnant to the touch.

She let the hours run by without doing anything, already tense because of the violation she was about to commit, but also resolved to carry it out. When it was about five o'clock and Saveria asked her if she needed anything, looking at her closely with her small, dark eyes, Matilde replied that it would be nice to have a cup of coffee. The coffee arrived, but she did not even touch it.

Saveria finally finished up her work and stopped to say goodbye. It was already dark outside—the livid darkness of nights that fall too quickly. Matilde got up, bolted the kitchen door and turned the key in the front door, leaving it askew in the lock in case Enea returned and tried to open it with his own key. Then she headed to the cupboard, took the keys for the rooms upstairs, and went down the hall. She picked out the biggest key, her hand squeezing the other one along with the thick brass ring holding them together, and inserted it into the door leading to the stairs. The lock released easily because Enea oiled it often, and the door softly opened.

The door leading to the second floor was always kept closed, in part so the heat would not escape during the cold season and also so the gusts of air from the storms in spring and summer would not slam it shut. At least that was how it was in the beginning, when Enea still had not moved all of his things little by little into the quarters over the lemon-tree room, like an enormous ant that was preparing its nest for the winter. Later on, the door had stayed shut simply because her son had wanted it that way.

The staircase was wide and protected by a banister whose curved handrail stood out black and shiny when Matilde flipped on the switch that lit up the large crystal chandelier. At the top of the stairs on the right there was another closed door, a very tall door with a dark painting hanging above it that depicted large, leafy trees and a castle in ruins. To open that door, Matilde used the second key.

She went into Enea's study. She knew she was all alone in the house, but felt acutely apprehensive just the same, as if someone might suddenly surprise her from behind. She turned on the floor lamp beside the table, which had a fan-shaped lampshade in pleated fuchsia silk and cast its light directly on the flat surface. Matilde was very careful not to touch anything. She ran her eyes over the piles of papers and books heaped up on the bookcases and shelves, barely distinguishing the outline of the furniture beyond the arc of light. Enea had chosen pieces to furnish the study according to a method, yet Matilde could not understand what principles might have inspired it. What he called a desk was in reality a rustic table for kneading dough, made out of a common wood that was not ennobled by the fact it dated back to the fifteenth century. A row of square drawers made its rough lines all the more ungraceful and heavy. In contrast, Enea had chosen a valuable piece for his chair, carved in the seventeenth century by Andrea Brustolon. It was made of boxwood, with designs painted in black lacquer, and its arms were like knotty tree branches held up by figures of putti. Besides the chair, the only piece of furniture that was not loaded with papers and books stood in a corner. It was a delicate desk from the late 1700s, which was made out of oak, with a birch veneer, and stood on six tapered legs. It was constructed by David Roentgen in the Neuwied workshops, and arrived in Tuscany, and in the Monterispoli home, at the turn of the last century.

Matilde had a moment's hesitation before she turned her eyes toward the tall reading stand that loomed just beyond the light like a human shadow, but she finally made up her mind. The drawing of the woman that had upset her so deeply was gone.

She headed slowly toward the second room, which had an overhead light that spread the cold white gleam of halogen lights Matilde detested. The neatness here was almost irritating. Except for the bulky, beige velvet bathrobe left on the back of a chair and the pair of slippers scattered far and wide, the workshop was as clean as an operating room. The faucets of the grit basin were shiny and tightly shut, the tools put neatly away. There were sharp tools of every size and type—awls, penknives, and gimlets. The ones that were not in their cases were arranged according to size, hanging on small hooks driven into the shelves that hung above the workbench whose surface had been wiped clean of any trace of wood shavings and chips.

After turning on the light Matilde stood still in the doorway. On the workbench there was a carved bust made out of reddish wood. The head of a young woman with her hair hanging down loose around her shoulders, a thin face that expressed suffering, the eyes sunken in their sockets. There was just a rough outline of the face, whereas the hair was entirely finished in an astonishingly careful way, almost as if each strand of hair had been carved one by one, so fine and soft it looked real. The hair was what suggested that the woman was very young. The empty eye sockets reminded Matilde of the ones in the female head by Adolfo Wildt on the dresser in her room. Yet, while that piece had a laughing expression, the face of Enea's sculpture seemed to scream out a death knell. Matilde was certain of it: the girl was no longer alive.

Enea's other works were heaped in the open chest that took up an entire corner of the workshop—elegant amphorae decorated in floral motifs that mingled with small horses with flying manes and oxen pulling plows, and little cherubs with their halos caught on a deer's branchy antlers.

Matilde looked again at the wooden sculpture of the girl sitting on the workbench, and it seemed as if those hollow eyes reflected her very own suffering.

Then she spotted the scalpels. Steely and cold, they were left on top of the workbench. Matilde ran the palm of her hand over her skirt, a gesture she habitually made when she was nervous and thought her hands were bathed in sweat. She was about to go back out of the room, telling herself that without her glasses she could not be sure those shiny instruments were actually scalpels, and Nanni's scalpels at that, but that woman's eyes would not let her. They implored her to do something so that other young women would not suffer like her.

Matilde went over and gathered up the scalpels one by one. Then she went downstairs, took the keys back into the kitchen and went to put the hateful scalpels back inside the case on the fireplace mantel.

17

Two days after the double homicide, when news of it broke, it was as if the entire city had been seized by some violent, collective emotion, charged with that bitter cruelty that is born from fear.

On the outskirts of the city, and in the homes located on the outskirts, people gathered to give their opinions on the stairs and in the hallways, in the doorways of grocery stores. In offices, they stood around the desks of the people who seemed to know more than the others about what was what. People summed up the facts excitedly, interlacing opinions and curses and indulging in a sort of instinctive self-defense, and ended up demonstrating that the guilty person was the sick offspring of some rich family (to whom past cases of syphilis and other obscure illnesses were attributed). They made up witty remarks and blood-chilling plays on words. They raved on that the killer might also be an Englishman of the nobility (maybe a descendant of that Prince Albert who, as everyone knew, was Jack the Ripper). He might have come to enjoy the city's good air and its silly-assed people, who were perhaps even showing him some fine hospitality in one of those old palaces on the hillsides.

On the other hand, the more well-to-do families arranged dinners and get-togethers that, in plain words, could be defined as events given "in honor of the Monster." The style was more contained and the words softer, but the results were more or less the same. They raved on here too, and with intentions that were even more malicious, often with the precise aim of spreading the seeds of misgiving around someone's name. A man was not able to live alone or to use razors or knives in his profession or trade without immediately being identified as the potential Monster.

A well-known gynecologist in the city, investigated a few years earlier for having seduced a young patient, was already being fitted for handcuffs. Some real brains even went so far as to claim there was reverse male chauvinism at work. Could the possibility that the serial killer might be a woman actually be ruled out? If someone objected that a woman would not have the physical strength to perpetrate those acts of carnage, the immediate response was that shooting straight into a car did not require any strength, and neither did cutting a corpse's flesh into pieces. Of course, but before being cut up the corpse was pulled out of the car and carried several hundred yards away. Dead weight is dead weight. All the same, weren't there women with muscles just as strong as a man's, and even stronger? There were women athletes, and mountain climbers too (at this point the person talking implied that he personally knew at least one) who were strong enough to lift not just one dead body, but two.

Everyone had their own Monster. If someone asked why they chose that person rather than someone else, they could only reply that their reasoning was incontestable. Was it really possible they did not realize it? The discussions went back and forth until late into the night, to be picked up again the following evening at the point where they had broken off.

People's imaginations ran wild over the fact that this time, for the first time, the killer had removed the victim's breast. Up until the last homicide, when he had made incisions on the young women's breasts, he had certainly followed the contours, but did not go so far as to mutilate them. In the past it had been written that the killer could be a "mama's boy," bound so tightly to the maternal figure that on the one hand, he nourished a morbid curiosity about the most distinctive symbol of motherhood, and on the other, a terror of touching it. When he brought himself to remove the breast, according to the experts, he finally freed himself of an old Oedipal complex. Instead, according to the most cynical ones, he had simply wiped out the image of a breast, the mother's, which must have been so withered up by then that it had to be thrown away.

The police had added reinforcements to the anti-Monster squad, deploying almost all of the officers on the force, and warned the citizens, the youngest ones most of all, not to go out late in the evening and not to stray beyond the populated areas and well-lit streets. Nonetheless, there were those who continued to wander around, despite the fact that the weather had turned cold and a biting wind had started to blow. Some people made themselves go with friends to the remotest parts of the outskirts just to relish telling others they had done it. Fear was everywhere though, and held the people in its grips.

Journalists from all over the world poured into the city, and people who had the chance to stand around and talk with one of them spouted hypotheses and opinions, and sometimes even names, without stopping to weigh their words. In any case, the Monster was a reality of the city, and if foreigners thought they could come and understand everything in the space of a few hours, they ought to learn that presumptuousness only leads to ignorance.

Thousands of copies of a poster hatched by city hall and the magistrate's office along with a group of psychologists were plastered all over the city walls. It had a huge eye on it and a warning written in four languages telling young people to keep their eyes open, with no mention of either the killer or the murders that had already been committed. Although the stated aim was to alert everyone, but not to alarm them, people on the street thought the posters were a multilingual tower of Babel, indecipherable even for the young people from the city, let alone for foreigners.

Prostitutes, transvestites, and Peeping Toms came in on their own to tell who they saw and who they met. Even if they were moved by a sincere spirit of collaboration with the police and by pity for the young victims, there were those in the homicide squad who suspected they did it in order to earn themselves some backing and leniency for the future. As if that were not enough, they kept the men who could have been used elsewhere tied up for entire days.

Special telephone lines were installed to gather information from people who wished to remain anonymous. There were so many calls, of such urgency too, that one night one of the officers assigned to the switchboard let it slip that he would have liked to be the Monster himself so he could rip out the guts of all those mythomaniacs.

From time to time, it was announced in tones rang-ing from consolatory to threatening that the State's po-lice chiefs were staying in constant contact. People re-marked that the State's police chiefs remembered them only on occasions when the Monster struck, and he would have done well to go do some cleaning up in Rome.

Although the killer who was murdering couples may have been just a theoretical problem for everyone else, he had become a very real torture for Matilde.

Matilde did not remember ever being so anxious to fol-low the news reported in the newspapers, not even dur-ing the war, and had never known before what was going on in the city down to the very last detail. When she read that the Monster roamed around dark paths with his imposing, faceless body, carrying the gun in one hand and the knife in the other, ready to strike down innocent lives, she felt as if she were dying.

That was how she imagined Enea when he went out at night, tall and imposing, his face engulfed by the shadows of night. By then she was telling him every lit-tle bit of information. As if that were not enough, every single thing her son did, every sentence he spoke, con-firmed or bolstered her suspicion in some way.

"It's enough to make you sick, reading these things," she told him one morning while they were at the table having breakfast. "The writing and descrip-tions are so well done it seems as if you can see that man right before your eyes."

Enea shook his head. "To write about him and de-scribe him, you'd need the pen of a Dostoyevsky, quite the opposite of that bunch of hacks. I don't know whether it's due to lack of skill or calculation, but it seems as if they're doing everything possible to feed people's sick fantasies. The man must have his reasons."

Matilde almost suspected her son was taking the killer's side. "Reasons?" she said, and then added categorically, "No reasons exist for what he does."

"Come on, Mama, try to understand. Civilized people don't demonize a human being that way, no matter how tainted with guilt he may be. It wasn't by chance that Dostoyevsky came into my mind."

"It almost seems as if you're putting those poor young people who were slaughtered and the man who slaughters them on the same level," Matilde burst out.

"In a certain sense, yes," admitted Enea. "They are all victims in the same way. Can you rule out the possibility that the killer might be a solid member of society, maybe a wonderful father and family man, who is so mentally disturbed that he is not aware of what he's doing? Perhaps he's overcome by homicidal rage that he certainly can't control. Then he forgets it happened."

"They say he lives alone," replied Matilde. "That only someone living alone would be able to escape discovery for such a long time. No mother, no sister, no father much less, and no brother would tolerate being around a person like that without at least trying to prevent him from harming someone."

"Alone?" Enea shook his head. "He lives with his mother. If he were alone, he'd already be lost in despair or would have betrayed himself. He wouldn't have been able to go on. He would have committed suicide or let himself be killed. I'm convinced he goes back home, to a mother."

"And the mother?" asked Matilde. "The mother would endure a son like that without doing anything?

At the very least, she would die of a broken heart." She added, "Then he would be left all alone."

"Mothers have a capacity to endure things that no other living being has, and each mother expresses love for her child in a different way. Not on the basis of an abstract conceptualization of maternal love, but according to her child's needs. How many times have you happened to hear some mothers comparing themselves to other mothers with a child who is insane, sick, or deviant, and say that they could never endure it? Then how many times have you happened to see mothers with a child who is insane, sick, or deviant not endure their misfortune?"

When Enea talked about certain things that she did not grasp, Matilde became nervous. "A mother also has civic duties," she declared. "If a son goes around slaughtering people, the mother must certainly make it a matter of conscience."

"Perhaps, but a matter of conscience will remain purely an ideal. No mother would ever turn in her son. If for no other reason than fear of the scandal. A mother could even hope he would be shot down by gunfire if this means putting an end to her suffering. Or she might wish he would die in a hospital bed from some horrible illness, but not without dignity, his body being treated but not his mind, because mental illnesses have no dignity at all."

Enea continued talking to his mother about the Monster as if he had thought a lot about him, and finally concluded, "No mother would ever turn in her own son, even if he were a killer, just to save other people's children. It would be unnatural. When they catch him, the so-called Monster will cease to be a monster. He'll have a first name and a last name, and also a face and a personal life. They will go digging into his existence as if the normality of having a name and a face would finally make him decipherable and quantifiable, like any other citizen. With the same identical yardstick, or rather, microscope. However, since the yardstick should be different, the numbers won't come out right. So once that ordinary citizen has been reduced to a carcass stripped of every last bit of flesh, he will be locked up in a criminal psychiatric asylum and bound to a restraining bed, condemned to definitive madness."

Matilde listened to her son's words as if every single one of them opened up a mental wound. She could not stop herself from thinking that Enea was referring to himself and her.

With effort, she struggled to ask, "But then what does a mother have to do?"

"Endure her son for what he is. Also because the mother of a monster must be a monster herself."

That night, Matilde dreamed her son was caught up in a tight circle of people who were cursing the killer. The only one to take his side was Enea. At a certain point, he started to run, and the others chased after him, yelling. He was overtaken, crushed by the people chasing him and left bleeding on the ground. A scalpel suddenly peeked out of one of his pockets, clinking as it fell onto the asphalt.

❦

"You can't understand. I tell you, you can't understand," exclaimed Nanda, looking askance at George Lockridge.

They were sitting in the Englishman's little yellow car in the Santo Giovanni Hospital parking lot. They

161

were waiting for Enea, who had gone up to get his test results. Nanda took long drags off her cigarette and held the smoke in her lungs for a few seconds before she blew it out all in one strong puff, filling the car with a pungent cloud. George rolled down the window a few inches, watched the smoke wedge through the opening, and closed it again.

"There's not much to understand," he said. "I warned Enea that it wouldn't last forever."

"Why don't you shut up?"

A woman with a large shopping basket brushed against the car door, turned to look at George, and cast a quick sign of apology. The Englishman swore under his breath.

"You must have your own problems too," he said after a short while, "but you're still almost a girl. Sooner or later you'll meet some man your own age, and good-bye Nanda."

"I told you to shut up."

A horn honked behind the small car. Lockridge looked in the rearview mirror and saw a car with a doctor's parking sticker on the windshield. He started the car and moved it to the side to let the other one pass by, and then went further ahead to park.

"If you want to know," Nanda resumed, flinging open the door to throw away the cigarette butt, "Enea is like a brother to me. In fact, even more. Like a father."

The Englishman laughed, and started to cough uncontrollably. "Don't come to me with theories of incest now." After a while he added, "If Enea didn't keep you supplied with money and dope, would you stay with him?"

Nanda thought about it seriously. "I don't know. Of course I hooked up with him because it was convenient. But that was in the beginning. Now I don't know any more."

"Close the door. It's cold."

Nanda closed the door and lit another cigarette right away.

"Enea is a real gentleman," said Lockridge after awhile. "You ought to meet his mother. You'd understand a bunch of things." He looked her up and down. "You know, don't you, that you can really hurt him a lot? You're the only person who can hurt him."

"You always talk too much, and at the wrong time."

Enea emerged from the glass door of the hospital. He looked around, and when he did not see the car where he had left it, he began to look worried. Then he spotted the yellow car and took off in that direction, the large yellow envelope with the test results flapping in one of his hands dangling at his side, his coat unbuttoned, and his yellow scarf hanging down all to one side. Nanda got out of the car and sat in the back seat.

"You didn't need to move," exclaimed Enea, hesitating in front of the open door.

"But you don't fit back here," replied Nanda. She kept quiet until George had started up the car again and gone out of the hospital gate, then said, "Take us to my house."

Surprised, the Englishman turned around to look at her. "What! Didn't we agree to go to Ponte a Ema?"

"I don't feel like it any more. Take us to my house I said."

When they arrived at via de' Renai, Nanda barely even said goodbye to the Englishman. She slipped through the doorway and waited for Enea to join her. Looking him straight in the eye with a serious expression, she said, "I don't want to see him anymore." She realized Enea was staring at her bewildered, and added, "He forces me to think."

Nanda was very nice that day. First she made coffee, and then she washed and dried the coffee cups. A few weeks earlier, Enea had given her a television, and she spent the days sitting on the floor to watch all of the shows. It was the first time she had had a television at her disposal. Since Enea had taught her to use the remote control she had stayed glued to it and spent hours and hours pushing the buttons for fear of missing something. That day, however, she did not turn it on. Nanda closed the curtains and took all of her clothes off. She went over to Enea and started to take his clothes off too. She took off his jacket, and then his tie and shirt. When she saw that he was wearing a woolen undershirt she burst out laughing. "My father doesn't even wear this stuff any more!"

Enea was not hurt because he understood that Nanda did not say it maliciously. Deeply moved, he let her continue. For a long time he had had the desire to feel his own naked body against hers, but he had never found the courage to ask. The fact that Nanda had sensed it filled him with wonder. His body moved softly in agreement as she slipped off his clothes, but he did not let her take off his shoes and socks. He did that himself.

Since the day she had sat down on the chair with her legs spread, thinking he would enjoy it, and he had run away, Nanda had not exhibited herself in those poses again. She sensed that she had seriously upset Enea, but she was sure that he would enjoy being under the covers with her, with both of them naked. And so it was. She lay down on top of his white, fleshy body, tickling him behind his ears, rubbing her cheek against his, guiding his hand along her own body. Enea kept his eyes closed and was careful not to breathe too heavily. Nanda flattened her body against him, then moved again, drawing away, and he opened his eyes wide, suddenly rolling over to look for her.

"You're afraid, aren't you? You're afraid I might leave," laughed Nanda. She dove on top of him.

That sort of lovemaking went on for a long time, as Nanda reached one orgasm after another and Enea, enraptured by seeing her enjoy such pleasure, anxiously moved his hands the way she had taught him, careful not to make a mistake, but to follow her body's different rhythms. When the young woman lay still against him, exhausted, Enea was uncertain for a moment. He moved his hand again, looking at her questioningly, but she had fallen asleep.

18

"If your glucose levels are too low now, it means you're not eating right," said Matilde when Enea told her the test results. "Right after you take your insulin shot you should sit down to eat, at least when you're home. You always take your insulin first thing when you get up, and before dinner in the evening, and you're hardly ever gone for breakfast and dinner. So I'd like to know how something like this could happen. Did you talk about it with Uncle Dono?"

"I talked about it with Morigi," answered Enea, who was helping his mother put the jars of pickled vegetables back in order on top of the kitchen cupboard. "Uncle Dono wasn't at the hospital the other morning. It seems he has a touch of the flu."

"I need to call him," murmured Matilde.

When they had finished putting away the jars, Enea started to leave. Matilde told herself she could not let him go until she asked him the question that she had been burning to have answered for over an hour.

"Was there a lot of commotion at the hospital?" she finally brought herself to ask.

"Commotion? The usual. Why?"

"Didn't you hear that the morning before last they found a bullet in the parking lot?"

Enea turned to look at her, waiting for the rest.

"A twenty-two caliber bullet," specified Matilde. "Exactly identical to the ones used by the Monster."

"They found it in the hospital parking lot?"

"Exactly. I heard it on the one o'clock news on the radio." Matilde turned to look at Saveria, who was at the sink washing the lettuce.

"Let's go sit down over there," she said. "It's impossible to talk here with the water running." In reality, she did not want Saveria to listen to what they were saying.

"I'm in a hurry, Mama."

"You can't be in such a hurry that you can't find two minutes to listen to your mother." Matilde walked into the living room and sat in a chair against the wall and pointed to the easy chair in the corner for Enea. She was determined to get to the very bottom of things. "A stretcher-bearer was getting out of his car, and the tip of his shoe hit a bullet that rolled away, catching his attention. He informed the police, and the ballistics test concluded that the caliber is the same as the one used by the killer."

Enea smiled slightly. "There's no need for a ballistics test to figure out the caliber of a bullet."

"Well that's exactly what they said on the radio."

"Then they said something stupid." Enea was starting to become irritated, and Matilde noticed he was raising his voice.

"At any rate, now they've gotten it into their heads that the person who lost the bullet may have gone to the hospital for some reason in the last few days. To visit a sick relative. Or to have tests done."

"You don't just lose bullets," Enea said flat out.

"Precisely." Matilde paused a moment. "The other

theory is that the killer might have wanted to throw out a challenge to the investigators."

Enea slowly got up from the chair, looking at his watch. "I really do have to go now."

Matilde thought it was very strange that her son left her that way, without asking her why in the world she was so interested in a thing like that. He did not even make a quick reply or comment on another fact—that he had been at Santo Giovanni Hospital two days before.

You don't just lose bullets, he had said.

In fact, the police were not at all convinced that the bullet had been lost. Someone, maybe a journalist, had advanced that theory, but it had been discarded. The killer had never left a trace, except when he had chosen to. No fingerprints had ever been found, or tire marks, or anything else.

A very big footprint, from a size twelve shoe, had been lifted near the camper with the two Germans, and they had said that the killer must have been about six feet two inches tall. The theory was based on the assumption that in order to shoot the way he had shot through the windows of the Volkswagen camper, and with a downward trajectory no less, the man was certainly well above average height. Enea had his shoes custom made because it was hard for him to find his size. There were few people as tall as he. Then someone had made the statement that the footprint had probably been left by an officer who had gone up to the vehicle without paying attention to the soft ground.

However, surgical gloves had been found.

A bullet had been found too.

᠅᠅᠅ ᠅᠅᠅ ᠅᠅᠅ ᠅᠅᠅ ᠅᠅᠅

Two challenges. The killer felt so invincible that he needed to compete, even on the field of the investigation, with the people hunting for him. Or else, as one psychologist maintained, he was beginning to feel worn out, and in his own way was asking to be stopped.

While going into the living room with Enea, Matilde had thought that if the conversation had proceeded calmly she would also have tackled the problem of the scalpels. It seemed as if Enea had not noticed that she had taken them from the workshop and put them back in the case on the fireplace mantel. For a couple of evenings, when he had gone up to the quarters over the lemon-tree room after dinner, she had expected to see him come back downstairs like a mad bull. The day when he had been totally beside himself because she had set foot in his study, and he had shattered the glass of the picture hurling the keys at it, came back into her mind. But Enea had not done anything, or said anything. As if he did not remember.

᠅᠅᠅

If someone had asked her, Matilde would not have been able to explain why she went to the funeral for those two young people who were killed a few days earlier. She took meticulous care getting ready, as she usually did when she knew she would be taking part in an important occasion. Even though the temperature was not cold enough to warrant a fur coat, when she stood in front of the open armoire she decided to wear her mink.

If anyone noticed her among the people crowded together in front of the church, they undoubtedly took her for a kind-hearted woman who felt pity over the tragic event. She stood up straight amid the other people, regretting that she had not brought even a single flower, holding her hands together, her eyes fixed on the portal from which the two caskets would emerge. The sun filtering through a light haze illuminated the features of her face, which could have appeared tense with emotion. Instead, she felt hard as stone inside.

She could not figure out her total lack of emotion. She had expected to be overcome with pity, or fear, or that acute sense of anguish that over the last few years would suddenly assail her, which made her think it was an ugly way to grow old. Rather, she felt as if she were a passerby who had happened along by chance. She was not aware deep down that she had gone there because she suspected her son of being the cause of that funeral service. She knew, though, that she had decided to attend because she felt it was right in a certain sense.

A few days after the funeral services, Matilde arrived at the conclusion that she urgently needed to talk with someone. She could no longer bear the idea of spending her days in solitude harboring that secret inside. Sometimes she had the feeling she was about to go out of her mind, and the only recourse she could discern was to have a calm exchange of ideas with a person who was able to understand. But she could not decide who the right person might be.

The first name that came into her mind was Calambrina Sensini. Calambrina had a profound way all her own of looking beneath the surface of things, sometimes managing to grasp their most hidden meanings with an acumen that Matilde found surprising. In the past she had often happened to think that friendship was precious, if for no other reason than because Calambrina always had an all-encompassing vision of each and every person and everything that happened, as if she could see them inside and out simultaneously. She imagined herself sitting on a wicker chair in the Sensinis' messy living room, with Calambrina in front of her, braiding and unbraiding her hair as she dug deep inside her, demanding precise words and clear concepts, looking her straight in the eye as if she wanted to strip her of her ideas. No, she was not willing to be stripped naked. She needed someone who could understand her state of anxiety and, at the same time, would be willing to listen to her without expecting to force her into the finality of saying certain things out loud.

She was surprised that he had not come to mind sooner. Andreino Colamele. Although she and Andreino saw each other rarely, their way of talking to each other those rare times had always remained the same, hovering between what was said and what was suggested, creating a form of communication that was more allusive than explicit, yet no less decipherable for the two people who possessed the key.

Matilde called to let him know about her visit, asking what time was most convenient. The notary replied that if she were to come around seven it would be best. At that hour the secretaries would already have left, and he did not answer the phone then. So they could talk in peace.

Matilde did not have any doubts about the wisdom of her choice. Andreino had understood at once the need for discretion about the appointment. In fact, he had set it for a time when there would be no witnesses who perhaps might be only too eager to tell Enea that his mother had come to meet with the notary.

19

Andreino Colamele did not think for a moment that Matilde wanted to see him in order to ask for technical advice related to his profession. When she needed his professional advice, she usually invited him to dinner, apologizing ahead of time because she would have to talk with him afterward about one of those "annoying darned things" that, she claimed, she could not make heads or tails of without his help.

Andreino thought he knew why Matilde had phoned. The fact that Enea had recently begun acting peculiar, to put it mildly, was, if not public knowledge, at least the talk of people who came to the office for some reason. Even if, as a rule, those directly involved were always the last to know what was going on, evidently a proverbial do-gooder had told the mother about her son's strange behavior.

Andreino had been the first person to react with disbelief when he was told that Enea was seeing a young girl of somewhat dubious virtue. His disbelief was due less to the fact that she might not be a good girl than to the fact that he would be seeing her at all. Until then, he had been firmly convinced that Matilde Monterispoli's son was not only a virgin, but also impotent.

In the past, the notary had also had episodes with women who were not exactly virtuous, and the fact that Enea might have an understanding with a shady woman did not disturb him at all. He was convinced, in fact, that the only relationships possible with women were the ones that were paid for. If at some point in his life he had taken into consideration the possibility of getting married to the daughter of some rich acquaintance, he did not even remember it now. He had never been one of those people who thought of marriage as a solution to financial and existential problems. For him, the objective had always been to own his own notary agency, possibly in the historical downtown area of the city. In order to reach that goal, he had worked with the notary Paola for over twenty years, saving him from the most disagreeable jobs, taking on the most difficult assignments, and also serving as his pimp.

Paola had been the one who taught him that women are only a stumbling block and had to be taken like a cordial, in one gulp and then away you go. Furthermore, the man must remain the absolute master in his own home. Women, he used to say, must be used as if they were the elixir of life—the more expensive it is, the more effective it is. When a man feels the need, he only has to find them and then forget them.

Engaged as he was in tackling the difficulties of acclimating himself (Colamele came from Palermo) and with the long hours he spent in the notary office, Andreino had given vent to his instincts, which were rather abundant among other things. He obeyed Paola's rules, and did not mind it. Andreino and the notary thus began to develop an understanding that had something conspiratorial about it. In the end, Paola had brought him into the agency as a partner, and later, when he died, Andreino became the sole owner.

There was just one memory that Andreino still could not explain clearly. It had to do with the period right after the war and the evenings spent in Nanni Monterispoli's home. He had regularly frequented their home through the years, but looking back over his past it was hard for him to understand whether those meetings with friends had influenced his development as an exile in a foreign land. However, they had clearly given him an education, namely, a deep knowledge of a certain class of people in the city. Through what Nanni and the others said he had acquired a sampling of attitudes and hypocrisies that had handed him the key to the ways he would act in the future.

They were all more or less rich, without any problems beyond the empty discussion of what was good and what was not, what was just and what was unjust (except for radically changing positions when the war was over and accounts had to be reckoned with the future). Thus, Nanni's friends had passed on at least one thing that was certain. Whatever they said, even the most serious things, had to be taken with a grain of skepticism. In drawing rooms, you had to go along with the people talking while keeping it firmly in mind that the things they would actually do would be different.

Sometimes Andreino was overcome by the doubt that, consumed as he had been by his concrete, personal problems, he might have let the vein of sincerity that undoubtedly existed in Nanni's and his friends' discussions slip by. Maybe, for the time those talks had lasted, they really had been a spectacular blaze that had burned up the old dry growth in the meadow to let the young grass grow stronger. After all, even after all those years the old people of the city still talked about those gatherings. The people who had not been at the discussions regretted it, while those who had been there boasted about it.

When he heard the office doorbell ring, Andreino went to answer it and had Matilde sit in his private office, avoiding the large room over Orsanmichele where he conducted business meetings. It was a sign of consideration. He had strangers go into the conference room, but only a few friends were allowed in his own office.

With an air of disgust on her face, Matilde pinched her nose between her fingers.

"These old buildings downtown still haven't lost the smell from the flood," she said. "You smell the mold as soon as you set foot inside."

"You're right to call it a moldy smell, but it isn't the flood's fault. It's the smell of old age," replied Andreino.

He sat down facing Matilde in one of the two chairs he kept in front of his desk, sensing that the large surface standing between them would have prevented her from feeling at ease. It would somehow have created a form of separation, establishing a professional relationship when there should not have been anything professional about it.

He kept quiet as he waited, aware that she was not a woman who lost time in useless chatter. But Matilde did not say a word. Andreino Colamele cleared his throat a couple of times, staring at her from beneath his furrowed brows, and he did not like what he saw. Could it be that Matilde was not well and had come to him to put some bequests in order? He had never seen her with such a pale, tense face. Even her hair seemed as if it had become thinner and whiter.

"Well then, Matilde," he brought himself to say. "If I weren't your friend, I'd ask you to what I owe this pleasure and so on. Since I am your friend, I'll simply ask what you are so worried about."

Matilde sighed, then stuck out her chin, a gesture that Andreino recognized as a sign she was gathering her courage.

"If I had to say what's worrying me," whispered Matilde, hesitating, "I don't know if I could find the right words. As for me having some worries at the moment, there's no doubt about it." Now she felt that it would not be easy to tell him about the anguish she felt.

Andreino respected her long, silent pause, and then he told her that she was undoubtedly there out of "motherly concern." There was no other person on earth, except for Enea, who could reduce her to that state of prostration. Matilde continued to be silent, so he went on talking.

"Believe me, I understand your anxiety," he said. "I don't know anything concrete about this matter. Yet if, as I imagine, Enea is doing things you don't like, then spending time with the wrong people must be to blame. Nothing can lead even the best man astray like keeping bad company. Enea has always devoted himself to abstract problems, to his research, so how can he defend himself from the traps life lays for each of us? Everything will straighten out though. You'll see. I'll talk to him myself."

Matilde looked at him as if she were surprised. When she made up her mind to have her say, it was to ask anxiously, "Bad company? Enea? What bad company?"

177

Andreino Colamele could have bitten his tongue for having been so rash. He tried to remedy the situation. "It's the first thing that comes to mind when a mother is worried about her son. That her son is keeping bad company. Just that."

Matilde's body stiffened defensively. He knew her well, so Andreino hastened to add, "Enea is a good boy, even though I shouldn't call him that any more. Still, for me he'll always be the boy he once was. Am I wrong, is he about fifty? Anyway, he works hard and does a good job. So good that when he decided to work just half days at my office, I was disappointed. Luckily, I didn't insist too hard to make him change his mind. With that horrible sick spell he had, I would have been sorry. Just one look at how bad he felt was enough for me to understand that he really couldn't go on. I was almost frightened. Luckily, thanks to your brother-in-law, Dono, the ambulance got here quickly. Speaking of Dono, I must say that he keeps close tabs on Enea. He phoned a couple of times to remind him to have his tests done. Who knows, though, if your son listened to him."

The mention of her son's health made everything simpler for Matilde. "It's true that he's not well. At night he stays awake until all hours and is constantly drinking water. . . . Then, sometimes, he seems possessed. You know how he has always been polite and calm. These days though, he raises his voice and gets all upset over every little thing."

Once she had started, Matilde could not stop herself. She told Andreino about the fit of temper when Enea had shattered the picture glass to pieces with the keys, and also about how he kept coming home late at night, after riding around God knows where on his moped.

~∞~ ~∞~ ~∞~ ~∞~ ~∞~

"With everything one sees and hears about in the city these days, I don't have any peace of mind at all. A lot of things are happening that never happened before. All of the bloodshed, all of those dead people. My son goes wandering around the streets, when there's a new moon and a full moon, when there's that kind of killer running around. How could I stay calm?"

Andreino Colamele did not say, even to reassure her, that the killer only had it in for young couples, and certainly not for men who were getting on in their years and not very desirable, like Enea. He did not say it because he thought he understood the meaning of the message that Matilde was trying to convey. He looked at his knotty hands, held palms up on his knees as if they were dead. Then he raised his eyes to look straight into Matilde's.

"Listen to me, my friend, at a certain age one has to beware of figments of the imagination, which attack treacherously, especially at night. If a person isn't careful, he risks being carried away by them. You're still young, relatively young at least. You can't let your nerves get the better of you and sink into morbid thoughts. Leave it to the people on the threshold of their eighties, like me. They doze just a couple of hours a night, so they lull themselves asleep with the thought of death. They thus relish its arrival with great anticipation."

He was aware of saying words that had no meaning at the risk of disappointing Matilde, but he needed to gain some time. The message she implied was so enormous that Andreino hesitated to give it the reality of a fully formed thought. After all, he was not even sure she meant exactly that. On the other hand, the reference to her son wandering around the streets when there was a new moon was too precise to possibly be casual. It seemed so crazy that a chill ran up his spine. He did not want to hear any more. Certainly Matilde would not go any further than what she had already said, but Andreino preferred not to run the risk of having to listen to anything more definitive.

He suddenly realized he could not bear Matilde's gaze any longer, which was motionless and fixed on his, as if it were lifeless. He stood up and went to open the small cabinet in the corner. Andreino pulled out a bottle of cognac, holding it toward Matilde to ask if she wanted some. When she shook her head no, he poured a small amount in a liqueur glass that he had taken out of the upper compartment.

He did not go back to sit down in the same chair. This time he went behind the desk, using the wide surface to sanction the very separation he had wanted to avoid earlier. Nonetheless, he said to himself, he could not send Matilde off without giving her the advice she had come for. Andreino Colamele was a notary down to his bones, and he would never have left a file outstanding.

"You see, Matilde," he said, carefully choosing each word, "the news is full of all sorts of crimes. Each crime is committed by a man, a man with social and family relationships that are inexorably marked by the discovery that the relative, or the friend, was capable of such a thing. But do you think that someone could foresee it, or prevent it? Each of us is responsible for his own actions, and those alone. Take the case of the so-called Monster. Maybe someone lives alongside him and suspects something, yet will never have solid proof. This is the meaning not only of the law, but of justice too. Solid proof. What would it serve to intervene, if not to tear two lives apart, instead of just one?"

"What if it could save some young lives?" objected Matilde.

"The young people you're talking about could save themselves, if they wanted to. If you're interested in knowing what I think about it, those girls would have done better to stay locked in their homes instead of wandering around isolated places at night. That way they would have avoided the worst."

When he saw that Matilde had no intention of replying, Andreino began talking again to affirm his disassociation from any allusion that might have been vented. "As far as Enea is concerned, I don't think he is taking so many risks after all. He's able to look after himself. He always has, hasn't he? He's a poet, but a poet with his head squarely on his shoulders, the likes of which are few and far between." Contradicting what he had said about Enea's inexperience a short while earlier, he painted a portrait in bold colors. Matilde's son emerged like some kind of new warrior, armed with a book but also with a blazing sword, able to understand but also to hold others at bay, willing to be tolerant but also to punish.

She understood that Andreino had understood. At that point, there was nothing else to say. But the notary had something to add. Setting his hands on the arm of the chair, he stood up, walked around the desk, and went to sit down facing Matilde again. This time the message had to arrive strong and clear.

"Have you thought about what would happen if that poor wretch, and I can only call him a poor wretch, were caught? If it's true, as people are saying around town, that he might belong to one of the old Florentine families, can you imagine the disgrace that would be perpetrated on what is perhaps an esteemed

family name? Can you imagine that name passing
people's lips? Bile, that's what would come out of their
mouths. Just because of one black sheep, one sick individual, one bad piece of fruit in a basket of good apples, they would be capable of destroying decades of
irreproachable conduct." He leaned toward her, whispering, "Who can say for sure that the ungodly drive to
kill hasn't burnt itself out? Calculating from the first
homicide, the killer ought to be about fifty by now. At
a certain point in its cycle the human organism has to
reconcile itself with age."

"I hope you're right," murmured Matilde.

When she left, she felt comforted. Yet again, Andreino had not disappointed her. There was certainly
not any solid proof. Furthermore, the murderer who
was killing the couples could actually start to be worn
out by age. Or some illness might intervene fatally as
the years went by.

In contrast, Andreino Colamele was very worried.
This time Matilde had dropped a problem in his lap
that he would happily have done without. The only
consolation he had at the end of that exhausting conversation was that nothing definitive had been said.

Enea certainly did not wear the attire of the new warrior that Andreino Colamele had transformed him
into, nor did he belong to that rare breed of poets with
their heads planted squarely on their shoulders, whose
image had blazed in the notary's office. Yet if something unusual happened around him he realized it.

He began by noticing that for some time Colamele
had been personally bringing him the assignments in

the morning for work that had to be finished up during the day. Then he lingered, staring at him with his old gaze, dull yet just as penetrating, and difficult to interpret. He also sat down on the corner of Enea's desk, which he had never done before, with his arms propped on the top and his shoulders bent over, wasting his time talking about things that had little if any meaning.

"When a person has the good fortune to belong to an important family, which is at once a rampart against the storm and, in a certain sense, a noble crown, he has duties, real dynastic duties. He receives, but in exchange, he must give. Every act of conduct must be irreproachable, such that it doesn't give cause for the shadow of a doubt, not even remotely."

Despite growing up among people who preferred to imply or insinuate, rather than to state or explicate, Enea had never learned to go beyond the strict meaning of words, which, in his opinion, were so rich, numerous, and exact that they could express any concept with precision. So he remained silent, waiting for Andreino Colamele to make up his mind to either talk more clearly or free him of his presence and let him work.

There was one topic, however, that the notary confronted explicitly, and perhaps even with excessive brutality. When he spoke about women, Andreino Colamele was incapable of mincing words, and with Enea he also dove straight in.

"I haven't always been old," he said, "and most of all, I'm not so old that I don't remember how much the flesh can make a person suffer if it isn't satisfied. But there are ways and then there are ways to approach the matter of sex. You're not all that young anymore either, and you have to admit that you're not even endowed with the kind of gorgeous looks that make women lose their heads. Intelligent, without a doubt, and also a distinguished gentleman, but have you ever heard of women hooking up with a man because they recognize his intelligence and refinement?"

One morning he suddenly came out with another stratagem.

"If there's more than a ten year difference in age" he said, "between a man and a woman . . ." Andreino Co-lamele had always been convinced that the difference in age between a man and a woman should not be more than ten years, an unconditional number for him. If someone asked him why, he just answered that that was how it was, period. If by chance the man was the one to wonder what kept a woman who was way too young by his side, then "if there's an age difference of more than ten years, the underlying motivation can only be money. As long as a person is aware of it and opens the purse strings when it's deemed opportune, everything is fine. Most of the time, however, women who are too young get the upper hand. Then the men lose control of the situation, perhaps exposing them-selves to obligations that are hard to absolve." Seeing that Enea continued to stare at him as if he were not lis-tening, he added, "Certain things must not be underes-timated. They're an explosive combination. They can make a person lose his psychological balance, and per-haps even his mind."

Enea guessed that Andreino must have found out about Nanda somehow and was trying to warn him. He spoke with the best intentions, Enea was certain of

it. However, he did not go beyond this certainty, because he thought the notary's arguments were not
worth the least effort to interpret.

"I understand, I understand," he mumbled every
now and then, continuing to hope that the notary
would stop.

20

The sense of comfort Matilde had believed she felt after the conversation with Andreino Colamele abandoned her before she even arrived home. On top of her own fantasies she now had the image of scandal evoked by the notary, with the consequent disgrace of the old family name, whose bearers had the sole fault of having begotten the Monster. She thought about it as an image because for her that entire story was represented in images, from the horrible photographs shown on the television and blown up on the pages in the newspapers to the black headlines printed on posters displayed on the newspaper stalls. Treacherously coupled with the image of scandal was also the image of the killer bound to a restraining bed in a criminal psychiatric asylum, as Enea had said the man would wind up if they caught him.

She thought about it so much that it seemed as if the two experiences had already come to pass, as if she had actually lived through them, with journalists laying siege on her home and shoving microphones up to her face while the people in the neighborhood pointed her out as the mother of the Monster. Then the long trial, with her name and Enea's displayed obscenely in every kind of printed material possible. Finally, she saw herself sitting in Nanni's easy chair and imagined a drooling creature, faceless and nameless yet bound to her by something that ran deep, who was held tightly by the coarse cloth of a straightjacket and immobilized on the metal bed by four straps, in a cell without any windows.

When they showed the composite sketch on the news, drawn by the police according to the description given by an eyewitness who maintained that he had caught a glimpse of the killer on the night of the last murder, Matilde was dumbfounded as she looked at it. The face was square, with small, close-set eyes and a low forehead that extended obliquely beyond the thinning hair at the temples. If she had had to say who it resembled, she would have picked Calambrina's husband more than her son.

Exactly one month after the last crime, something else happened. A second bullet was found under the mailbox near a post office in the same neighborhood as Santo Giovanni Hospital, where the first bullet had been recovered. What Matilde referred to by then as "the scandal" started to well up again. The second bullet was also the same identical caliber and the same identical brand as the bullets used by the killer and the one that was recovered in the hospital parking lot. This time there was not any doubt. It was clearly a second message. By now in his fifties, the person who was guilty of the crimes was both physically and psychologically tired, worn down by the prolonged tension, and unconsciously desired to be stopped in his convulsive race to death.

Only one newspaper formulated a different theory. The killer perhaps lost the first bullet in the hospital parking lot out of carelessness. Without him noticing, it could have dropped in the car the night of the murder while he was loading the gun, and as he got out his foot inadvertently knocked it out. Now he was trying to muddy the waters by letting them find a second bullet, again in the same part of the city.

The post office was not the one in San Domenico di Fiesole. One day though, when a large certified envelope had arrived for Enea, and Matilde and Saveria were out, the mail carrier had left a card with instructions to go to pick it up there. Enea had taken care of it personally, saying it was on the same street as the hospital anyway, an area he knew like his own backyard.

Matilde kept staring at the description of the bullets, the year they were made and their brand. Something was hidden in the recesses of her mind, but she could not put her finger on it. It stirred deep within, affirming its own existence, but Matilde was unable to identify what it might be or what exactly it concerned. One of the pieces of news she had just read, undoubtedly. It must have struck her without her noticing and had begun to work stealthily on her mind while she continued to thumb through the newspaper.

She decided not to think about it any more. Yet from that moment on something about her behavior changed. In the morning she stayed in bed with the covers pulled clear up to her chin, her eyes closed, pretending to enjoy the sleep that would not come, until Enea had finished breakfast and left. The first times it happened, her son sent Saveria to check if he should wait for her, but in the course of a few days the novelty of the event wore off, and it became routine. When Saveria asked her if she was not feeling well, Matilde answered that she was not able to sleep the way she used to, and dozed off in the morning just when she should have been getting up.

Her mind drifted away during conversations, following the sounds of the words but not their meaning.
She began taking half a sleeping pill in the evening to
spare herself the pain of staying awake with her ears
straining to hear the sounds from the quarters above
the lemon-tree room. She forgot what needed to be
done and where she put things. She complained about
it at dinner one evening. Enea replied, "If I'm not mistaken, you've started gulping down a bunch of garbage
before you go to bed. You're old enough to know how
to take care of yourself. Besides that, you pride yourself
on knowing a lot about medicine. I want to remind
you just the same that sleeping pills block mnemonic
processes."

"It's easy for you to say," replied Matilde. "If people
don't sleep, they feel bad during the day, and can't do
what they should. Half a sleeping pill is better than
spending the night with your eyes staring wide open in
the dark."

"The further on in years one gets, the less need
there is to sleep," declared Enea. "Don't think I sleep a
lot either. I make do with those couple of hours I get."

Even weeks later, the newspapers were still dedicating
part of the first page to the discovery of the bullet.
Through a new reconstruction of the murders, they arrived at another theory. The killer tended to use the
cartridges sparingly. To kill his sixteen victims, he had
used fifty bullets in about thirty years. With the city in
a state of emergency, and the constant inspections of
gun stores and weapon factories, he must have been
afraid that his supply would be cut off at any moment.
This would have explained why he used the knife for

the first time on the body of a young man, the one killed at the Boschetta who was finished off with ten stab wounds.

The criminologists and psychiatrists had completed their reports and now proclaimed that the man suffered from a "distorted Oedipal complex." This was demonstrated by the ambivalent attitude shown toward the female figures and the antagonism shown toward the male figures. The detail that the young couples were attacked before the act of lovemaking was consummated also demonstrated that he could not accept the sexual act, and therefore it had to be prevented. Yet perhaps the man also did not know the mechanics of actual sexual coupling and mistook the preliminaries of lovemaking for intercourse.

There was a strong, insistent emphasis placed on the fetishes. Where did he preserve them? The fact that the man sectioned the pubis and breast, limiting the incisions to the cutaneous layer could only mean he devoted himself to real practices of fetishism. He prepared the remains for preservation and knew that fat does not keep, even in alcohol or formalin. In any case, some strips of fatty tissue were actually found at the site of the last homicide, as if the man had discarded them within view of the macabre operation.

There were numerous leather tanners and hunters in the region who were used to "mounting" their trophies, and the man could belong to one of those two groups. But surely not, the psychologists maintained, for without a shadow of a doubt the picture that emerged from the experts' reports and the inquiries was of a cultivated person who did not read pornographic magazines, but rather, erotic literature. Some of the titles were even cited. *The Amorous Adventures of Prince*

Mony Vibescu by Apollinaire and the *Collected Works* by the Marquis de Sade.

Enea decided to make the phone call from the café just down the street from the office. The idea that the notary's head secretary could listen to him bothered him, and George did not have a phone in his shop. The place was packed with people. The cashier knew Enea and was aware that he worked in the agency owned by Colamele, the notary with the office just around the corner, and stared at him while he maneuvered the telephone token and the receiver. When she noticed Enea was looking back at her though, she immediately looked away.

"Hello? Hello, Calambrina?"

"Don't tell me it's Enea!"

"Yes, it's Enea." He suddenly regretted making that call. He was simply trying to dump the burden that he should have shouldered into the lap of his mother's friend.

Calambrina sensed his hesitation and said, "Since you're calling, it means you're fine. So what's wrong? Is something wrong with Matilde?"

Enea answered that perhaps he tended to make too much of things, but in his opinion, his mother was going downhill at a troubling rate lately. Could Calambrina find an hour to go visit her and convince her to see a doctor? The woman promised she would, but when he hung up, Enea did not feel any calmer than before.

He went into the elevator to go up to the office and closed the glass doors. Enea stood undecided for an instant, then opened the doors again. For the first time

since he had been working for Colamele he decided to
skip work that morning. The interest he had always
felt as he solved problems the notary entrusted to him
had waned lately, and his employer's attitude made
him tense besides. The atmosphere in the office had
changed decidedly. He went out to the street, hesitated
a moment, but had a clear idea in his mind about
where to go. He headed toward via de' Renai.

As he rang at the door of the studio apartment and
heard the key turn in the lock, he got ready to smile,
but a scruffy young man appeared in front of him. He
was completely naked when he opened the door, and
then ran and jumped back between the sheets next to
Nanda. Enea stood in the doorway with the door wide
open, while the young woman lifted her head off the
pillow.

"Why are you standing there stiff as a board?" she
yelled. "Come on inside. The cold air is getting in."

Enea went inside and closed the door, but he remained standing, with his back against the door.
Nanda noticed the expression on his face and snorted,
and finally jumped out of bed. She was completely
naked too. She suddenly threw back the covers and said
to the young man, "Take off. The master of the house
is here."

The boy swore under his breath, but got up. He
took just long enough to throw on four pieces of dirty
clothing and then he left, saying goodbye to Enea with
a slight wave of his hand and slamming the door behind him.

"Do you want a cup of coffee?" asked Nanda, putting on the red dressing gown he had given her when
she was in the clinic.

Enea did not answer. So Nanda asked, "How in the world is it that you came by at this hour in the morning? Shouldn't you be at work?"

A syringe, a teaspoon, and half of a lemon were on the table. Nanda realized that Enea was looking at them. "That stuff ought to be enough for you to know that nothing happened," she muttered. "We shot up last night, got sleepy, and went to bed. We slept until you got here. Mario was cold, it was late, and he didn't know where to go."

Enea still did not say anything, so Nanda moved into the small kitchen, pretending to make coffee. She opened the dirty coffee pot, moving sluggishly, dropped the coffee grounds in the sink, and squeezed them against the porcelain. Meanwhile, she looked at the small dish rack in front of her without really seeing it. Then she turned toward Enea and stood in front of him.

"If you really want to know," she murmured, "I wish I was dead."

"I don't know, I don't know any more," said George, looking at Enea over the rims of his glasses. "I have always maintained it's better to die than to be alone, but maybe there's a limit to everything. If only you could . . ." He studied the expression on his face and shook his head. "But you can't."

They were in Gino's restaurant, and the Englishman was shoveling huge spoonfuls of beans up to his mouth, bending over the plate as if he were afraid it would run away.

"Yes, there has to be a limit to everything," he resumed, squashing the beans against the roof of his mouth with his tongue so he could avoid using his teeth. "But what do you think you'll do? You've known what Nanda was ever since you met her."

Enea felt sad, more than anything else, and upset by a sense of inadequacy. He looked at the Englishman as if his friend could help him see things more clearly. Yet he already knew that all of his observations would actually refer more to George and Luca than to him and Nanda.

"Can a man even accept things he doesn't understand?" said Enea. "Because I don't understand."

"And necessarily so. You don't understand because you commit the error that so many people make. You want to relate to the behavior of someone who is very different from you, and therefore from your own level of culture and upbringing. For Nanda, being discovered in bed with some young man is probably as normal as eating these beans is for me."

"But she said she wished she were dead."

"She was probably sincere, but in that moment and just for that moment," replied Lockridge. "She was really being herself only before, when she went to bed with that guy, and afterward, when you left. It's clear that when she's with you she tries hard to be not what she is, but what you would like her to be."

"What should I do?" asked Enea.

"Nothing. You shouldn't do anything. Leave the decision up to chance. It will decide things, don't worry." George stopped eating, sat in silence for a while, and after a few seconds added, "How often does a person leave no stone unturned, think ahead, and make plans, and then some opportunity suddenly comes along that for better or worse turns everything upside down?"

21

"Doctor! Doctor!"

Dono Monterispoli pretended he had not heard and quickly opened his car door. Out of the corner of his eye he had glimpsed Calambrina Sensini come out of the Riccardiana Library and preferred not to talk with her. Not only was he coming out of his lover's house on via de' Ginori, a busy road where a person always ran into someone, but he had never liked Calambrina. In fact, he could say he detested her. She dressed inappropriately for a woman of her age, overflowing with shawls and frills and wearing ridiculous dyed wool caps on her head. She also had such a brutally direct way of saying things that she unfailingly irritated him.

He climbed into the car and put his arm out to close the door. By then Calambrina had caught up with him and was sticking her head inside. "Doctor," she said, panting from the run, "I really do need to talk with you."

Dono Monterispoli automatically moved to get out, and once he was outside of the car he even struck a slight bow, but then stood stiff and detached as a dead herring.

"Doctor, I have to tell you that I'm very worried about Matilde and Enea."

With both of them standing at the side of the car, they were in the way of the other cars, which kept laying on their horns and brushed by within a few inches of them. They moved over to the sidewalk. The wind turned Calambrina's face red, making her features stand out even more.

"Matilde is worried about Enea," continued the woman, "and Enea is worried about Matilde, but they don't talk to each other. So things drift on, as if out of inertia, and are getting worse. I don't know how it will end. But one thing is for sure, it won't end for the better."

Dono Monterispoli let his eyes wander over the front of the houses, accentuating his detachment. When he wanted to, he could be extremely arrogant. "I'm afraid you really must explain what you mean more clearly," he murmured.

"Come on, Doctor, don't pretend you don't understand. You know very well that Matilde and Enea's living together isn't normal. I'd even go so far as to say it's unhealthy. As with any anomalous situation, it provided its own compensation up to a certain point, at least on the surface, and as time passed it started to exhibit problems. Enea called to let me know his mother isn't well. So I go to visit his mother, and she talks to me about her son and his strange behavior."

For the first time since they had begun talking Dono Monterispoli looked Calambrina in the eye and asked politely, "What would you propose?"

The woman began to fret away at her braid, on the verge of losing her temper. She felt the same dislike for Monterispoli that he had for her, and if she had not had Matilde's well-being at heart she would already have showered him with insults. "If I could propose something," she said, "it would be to separate them immediately. I'd send Enea off somewhere, to another city, and have Matilde take a long cruise. But since it's not up to me to decide, I'm asking you to intervene."

"Who? Me?" Dono Monterispoli lightly shook his head, giving just a slight smile of surprise.

"I feel like something's going to happen," said Calambrina. She hated exposing herself to Monterispoli's scorn, but she was unable to hold back. "You won't believe me, but I sense things. Sooner or later something is going to happen. I'm sure of it." She did not dare tell him that she had read tarot cards the night before, and death had appeared twice in Matilde's future.

"You're a very good person to be so concerned about my sister-in-law and nephew," said Dono, "but believe me, out of generosity you tend to make too much of things. Look at the situation in the light of reason. Matilde is a fulfilled woman, satisfied by a quiet life and motherhood. Enea is a cultivated man with a job that engages him and a cozy home where he can feel free to do as he pleases. Certainly he has some physical problems that aren't exactly minor, but they're being closely monitored. Don't worry, Signora Sensini, nothing is going to happen."

And with another bow he walked away and went to slide into his car.

∿◌

The headline banner displayed at the newspaper stand waved something that Enea caught out of the corner of his eye. Drug addict jumps off Ponte Vecchio into the Arno River. He did not connect the headline with Nanda, nor could he have. Since he had not read the newspaper, he had automatically thought the term *drug addict,* without any words indicating gender, referred to a male. But even if he had read it, he still would not have connected the suicide with Nanda. That some Ferdinanda Colucci might have preferred to drown in the river rather than live the life she lived would not have made him feel upset or anything else but a general reaction of pity. For Enea, Nanda was Nanda. He did not even know if the woman had ever told him her last name, and certainly he would never have connected it with Ferdinanda.

So he went to look for her without knowing she was dead.

He was supposed to meet her at three o'clock in Piazza Signoria to take her to the clinic for an exam with the liver specialist. For a while Nanda had begun having problems with her liver again and could not keep any food in her stomach. Enea had had to insist so that she would make up her mind to see a doctor, and he had finally convinced her. He had not seen her for two days because he had needed to leave Florence and accompany Colamele to draw up a preliminary sales contract at the bedside of an invalid. However, the agreement with Nanda was clear.

At four o'clock she still had not shown up. Enea did not start to worry until four-thirty. Even keeping in mind Nanda's habitual lateness, that much time was unusual for her. Probably, Enea thought, when she had agreed to let him take her to the doctor she actually believed what she was saying, but then she had changed her mind, as often happened with her.

He paced back and forth another ten minutes, and went into a café to drink a glass of warm milk, staying glued to the glass door so he could see if Nanda popped up somewhere. Then he went out again and started to walk around the square. When it turned five o'clock, he was numb with cold, and his legs and back ached. By then they had missed the appointment with the doctor, and he would not have known where to look for Nanda. He did not feel like starting to beat about the city far and wide, and he was certain that after that nasty little trick she would not stay on via de' Renai where he could find her.

He did not feel like going back home, imagining his mother's surprise at seeing him appear at that hour. He did not know where to go, so he finally decided to take refuge at San Domenico. As soon as he arrived he would go straight up to his study.

When he got there, he discovered that Matilde was not at home. Saveria was there, and ran up to him, putting a slip of paper in his hand.

"A certain Signor Mazzacane called three times," she exclaimed, satisfied that she could finally give him the message. "He says it's urgent and you have to call him right away at this number."

Enea went into the living room to make the call. Someone answered at the other end of the line, and in a hushed voice asked, "Hello, who's calling?"

"This is Monterispoli," said Enea. "May I speak with Signor Mazzacane?" He was certain he had called Aldo Mazzacane's office at the county hall.

When he came to the phone, Aldo only said softly, "Did you hear about Nanda?"

"No, what?"

The brief pause that followed seemed like an eternity.

"She's dead," said Aldo finally. "I'm here at her parents' house. If you want to come over too, they would be happy to meet you."

Enea arrived half an hour later. The streets were full of traffic, and it was stop and go as the taxi inched forward. The home was located on the outskirts, on via Menabrea in a small, modern, four-story building with a little garden in front and flowers on the balconies.

Nanda's mother, a slender, well-dressed woman, came to answer the door, not a single tear in her eyes. "Please come in and make yourself comfortable." She showed him into the living room, which was furnished with pieces of imitation Chippendale, their surfaces dotted with brightly polished silver trays and coffee pots. The large window was veiled by sheer curtains, topped by a valance of red damask velvet that matched the fabric on the chairs and sofas.

As soon as he saw him, Aldo Mazzacane went over to shake his hand. The gray-haired man sitting in the corner of the couch remained motionless, staring at Enea without saying anything.

"We know how much you did for our daughter," whispered Nanda's mother, "and we're grateful to you."

Everyone sat down. After a few minutes of silence the woman stood up to go get a bottle and four glasses from the liquor cabinet, whose interior was finished with mirrors.

"Did you read the papers?" Mazzacane finally asked Enea. When Enea shook his head, he went on, "Then you don't even know how it happened."

Enea shook his head again, and Mazzacane spoke softly, constantly looking over at Nanda's father as if he were afraid he would become upset. "The day before yesterday she left her house at about three in the morning. A neighbor woman who'd gotten up to drink a glass of water heard her. She must have headed straight for Ponte Vecchio, because at seven o'clock yesterday morning the body was found several miles downriver. She had put her identification card in a plastic bag, along with her parents' phone number. That's how they identified her so quickly."

"Where is she now?" asked Enea.

"At the morgue." Aldo Mazzacane lowered his voice even more. "They'll have to do an autopsy."

Enea held on for the three days before the funeral by spending a lot of time at Nanda's parents' apartment and walking about the city streets at night. At dawn he went back home for a couple of hours, then went out again. He attended the funeral services at the cemetery, standing apart from the others, his eyes lost amid all the tombstones following one after another. The only people there were himself, Aldo Mazzacane, her mother and father, and a young woman who had gone to school with Nanda and lived on the floor above them. He had come with a small bouquet of daisies, thinking he would toss them on the coffin, but then he handed the flowers to Nanda's mother.

When they headed toward the exit gates, Enea declined Aldo Mazzacane's invitation to go have something to drink. He stopped a taxi that was passing by and had it take him to via de' Renai, where he stayed shut up for two days and two nights, sitting in the chair near the bed. Both wakefulness and sleep clouded his mind, robbing his sense of the hours passing by. The morning of the third day, when he heard someone knocking at the door, he had to make an effort to stand up. His body ached and it was hard for him to walk. He opened the door like an automaton, and saw George Lockridge in front of him.

"I was sure I'd find you here," exclaimed the Englishman. His eyes were dull and his face was drawn from being so tired. "Why didn't you let me know what had happened? A young man who happened into the shop told me about it this morning. I called you at home right away, but I only got your mother. She's at her wits' end because she doesn't know where you have been. Luckily she still hadn't decided to contact the police. Come on, I'll take you home to her."

22

After Nanda's death Enea quit going to work at Colamele's office. He spent the days and also a good part of the nights in the quarters over the lemon-tree room, or else he shut himself up in his bedroom, only coming out late in the morning and going immediately back upstairs.

Matilde, on the other hand, started to get up early again and have the breakfast table prepared for two. Then she sent Saveria to call Enea through the door of his bedroom or the study. When her son did not come for breakfast she had a tray taken to him, with milk and some slices of toasted bread. She drank half a small cup of espresso, letting the rest of it get cold in the coffee pot, and then she told Saveria to clear the table.

She would sit in the chair in Nanni's study for hours, looking out at the gray winter days beyond the window. The branches of the trees were bare, and Matilde caught herself counting them one by one, comparing them to human fingers. One morning, including all the branches, large and small, she counted enough for ten hands. Another morning she counted enough for twelve and promised herself that sooner or later she would check which number was right. If someone called she had them told she was not there,

203

and she had stopped giving orders to Saveria, leaving it up to the woman to decide what to do and what to buy.

Calambrina rapped on the kitchen windows three mornings in a row. When Saveria repeated that the mistress was out, she loudly exclaimed, "Tell the mistress of the house that when she thinks she'll be in, she knows where to find me."

For some while, Lockridge had taken to coming by the house with a certain frequency. The first time he had come in, ignoring Saveria, and had slipped into the living room. Matilde suddenly found him standing right in front of her, bundled up in an old, brick-red coat, with a thick scarf of coarse wool wrapped around his neck.

"I came by to see how you both are," he mumbled, keeping his eyes lowered, as if he were embarrassed to look her in the face.

"You're very thoughtful," she replied icily. "We're very well."

"It would put my mind more at ease if I heard it from Enea," George responded, and without another word he headed toward the door that led to the stairs to the second story.

When Matilde heard him come back down, the entire morning had gone by, and Lockridge did not stop in to say goodbye to her. From that day on, the Englishman began to drop in at all hours. He would come in and go straight upstairs free as he pleased, as if Enea had given him the key to the house.

Some nights Enea was overwrought, and he yelled and sobbed, throwing everything he happened to lay his hands on. Matilde lay still in her bed, listening to the sound of things thudding on the floor one after another, and telling herself over and over again that she had to make up her mind to do something. Sometimes Enea's voice and Lockridge's were so low that she could not catch anything but a whisper, but other times her son's voice rose loud enough to come through the walls. Then she heard the curses and the swearing, directed at some entity that was not identified but that had to be above everything and everyone if it could mete out just as much pain as it pleased and with such impunity.

Saveria went around the house as if someone had died. She spoke in a very hushed voice and walked on tiptoe. When she crossed paths with Matilde she stood aside, waiting until she passed by.

Enea always came for dinner shaved and with a clean shirt on and ate a few spoonfuls of soup and some vegetables half-heartedly without saying a word, his eyes staring off into space. Then he would stand up and push his chair in, dragging it along the floor, mumble some parting words, and go up to his study again.

One morning Matilde made the decision to talk to him. For the entire night, she went over the little talk she was going to give him, determined to confront her son. She went to the end of the hallway, opened the door, banging it loudly so that the sound would travel, and went upstairs, stomping her feet on the stone stairs. She wanted Enea to hear her coming. If her son did not open the door for her, she would tell him in no uncertain terms that as long as she was alive this house was hers, and no door could be locked in her face.

Enea cracked open the door before Matilde reached the top step, slipped out, and closed it again behind him. He was wearing the velvet bathrobe, and his eyes had red circles around them.

"I'm coming right away, Mama. I won't ask you to come inside because there's an incredible mess in there."

They went downstairs together, but he did not follow her into the living room. He went into his bedroom first to make himself presentable. When he came back out he was wearing a jacket and tie, and a white shirt with narrow stripes.

They were silent for a few minutes, the mother sitting on a chair with a high, hard back, and the son perched on the edge of a chair. Enea was the one who spoke first.

"I realize that I have put you through some long, difficult days," he murmured. His voice was calm, resigned, and absolutely detached. "But you have to believe me when I tell you that I couldn't help it." He looked at her as if asking her to try to understand, and then he added, "I'm miserable."

Overcome by a sudden rush of emotion that she could not control, Matilde had to muster all her courage.

For the first time after so many years, she took a close look at her son, and saw a man with swollen eyes, the skin of his eyelids withered, wrinkles all about his round mouth, and stooped shoulders. As often happened when he was sitting, Enea let his arms dangle down between his knees, in a position that made him even bulkier than usual. He had a vulnerable look about him, like people who have suffered too many of life's assaults to be able to endure any more.

"I don't feel well," continued Enea, without taking his eyes off his mother. "I've neglected myself these last few days, and when I'm up in my study I often happen to get dizzy and become soaked in sweat." He lowered his eyes. "Don't think I'm telling you about my troubles to gain your pity. Try to understand. If I made you suffer in some way it's not because I don't care about you, but because I really could not help it."

Despite what she saw of the man Enea, for Matilde it was as if she had the baby born to her fifty years earlier in front of her, unable to look after himself and lost when she was not there.

"You've always loved your father more than me, haven't you?" was the only thing she could say.

Enea leaned forward as if to hear her better, since he was so surprised by the question that he thought he had not understood correctly. It finally registered and he replied, "They were two different kinds of affection that certainly can't be measured in terms of being more or less." He paused, then whispered, "A person can love in so many ways, Mama."

"I only loved one way," replied Matilde. "I loved you and I loved your father to the utmost possible, and I don't know any different kinds of love."

She got up to run her hand over Enea's head, and noticed that his hair was damp with sweat. "Now go and freshen up. I'll wait for you in the dining room."

As she headed off, Enea took hold of her wrist to keep her there. "If we could begin living again as we lived before, what kind of a life do you think it would be?"

Matilde looked at him silently for a few minutes and then, thinking carefully before she said each word, she answered, "This is the only kind of life I know. Do you have some other kind to propose?"

Saveria showed how pleased she was to see them together again by bringing a pitcher of orange juice and a small basket of apples to the table, which neither Matilde nor Enea touched. While they drank their coffee, the mother and son felt they had said everything they had to tell each other.

❧❧

"Is there anything warm for a poor old man to drink?"

Matilde started, whirling around toward the door of the dining room. She had not heard a sound, and the appearance of George Lockridge at a moment when she had the feeling she had cast the seed of possibility for a future deeply irritated her. Lately her dislike for the Englishman had turned into hostility. That he could come and go in that house as he pleased seemed to show an intolerable lack of respect. As soon as she saw him, she told herself that, at least in his case, she had to put an end to the surprises. Enea, instead, looked happy about the visit. He invited him to sit down at the table and asked Saveria to bring another cup. They sat for a long time without talking, while Lockridge slowly sipped his coffee and took a piece of toasted bread and dunked it in the coffee to soften it up.

"I'm pleased to see you two together," he said at a certain point, casting a glance up and down Enea, but without looking at Matilde. "How do you feel now?"

Matilde understood that he was not talking about her son's health, but about some secret that she was not aware of. "Enea isn't well," she declared. "He needs to take care of himself and to start doing something again. The notary Colamele would be happy to take you back to work with him."

Lockridge heaved a sigh and finally turned in her direction. "You've always tried to smooth the way for your son. Sometimes mothers, and friends too mind you, have to know when to stand back. A man has to be free to live through his own pain and to make the only kind of life for himself that will allow him to bear it."

"What pain, for heaven's sake!" exclaimed Enea, and she understood that breaking it off that way carried a hidden message for the Englishman. She was even more convinced of it when George changed the subject.

Enea and Lockridge decided to go out together for a walk, despite the heavy rain that streamed through the garden and beat against the magnolia leaves, making them rustle. Matilde did not say anything, but when Enea went to get his raincoat, she held out her hand palm up, almost putting it right up in front of Lockridge's face. He looked at her hand, raised his eyes to Matilde's face, and then looked back down at her hand.

"The party's over, eh?" he finally said.

"I wouldn't exactly call it a party," was Matilde's reply.

George Lockridge rummaged in his coat pockets, pulled out the keys to the gate and to the door of the house, and dropped them on Matilde's palm.

"You won't believe it," he said finally, "but I was only trying to help your son. I have the presumption to think that if I hadn't been there it would have ended up worse."

❧

Enea and the Englishman walked closely together, sharing the umbrella, which did not cover them. Enea's left shoulder was numbed from the cold rain. Lockridge could scarcely keep the rain from getting his face all wet.

"Are you going back to work at Colamele's?" asked the Englishman at a certain point.

"I don't know, I don't think so," answered Enea. "I haven't even thought about it."

They were going toward the city, walking downhill on viale Volta. The cars passed by, splashing water all the way onto the sidewalk, and some boy was running toward the bus stop with the hood of a red and yellow slicker pulled over his head.

"Your mother would like you to," said Lockridge, "but if I were you, I'd think it over this time. You're not the type to sit rotting behind a desk. If you want to know what I think, you ought to live on your own and only do the things that interest you. You only have one life, and you've already lived a good part of yours. At a certain age, you can't let the days slip by anymore. You have to enjoy each one, because it might be the last."

Enea stopped, turning to look at him with the expression he got when he felt that he was misunderstood.

"I wasn't sorry I worked at Colamele's office," he said. "But that's not the point. The point isn't even whether to live alone or with someone else. As long as Nanda was there, I thought a lot about living with her. I had also imagined asking Saveria to move in with Mama and spend the nights there. Now though, do you think it even matters to me where I live and with whom? The problem now is just living."

23

Matilde became aware that spring had arrived one morning when she opened her bedroom window and as she looked toward the hill, she saw the white flowers of the almond trees below the Badia Fiesolana. She stared at them for a few moments, as if they were an inexplicable wonder. She had hardly noticed the winter months passing by, and the unexpected warm air seemed oppressive.

She called Saveria to tell her that on the following Monday they would start the cleaning, beginning with the windows. With the sun shining, the windows looked filmy and iridescent, and the frames had become yellowish. They cut up old sheets and remnants from unworn undershirts for rags, and Matilde phoned the grocer to order a new supply of household cleaners.

For two weeks, mattresses and blankets were exposed along the windowsills, and rugs were laid out facedown on the lawn. The wood floors smelled of wax, and the sharp odor of ammonia in the kitchen made the air smell like a hospital. Everything was finally sparkling, even in the most hidden corners. Except for the quarters above the lemon-tree room.

"Ask Signor Enea when you can clean his study,"

said Matilde to Saveria one morning, her tone leaving no room for objections. Nonetheless, the woman gave the answer Matilde had tried to avoid.

"Why don't you ask him yourself? You know that Signor Enea is quick to say no to me."

"You're going to ask him just the same," insisted Matilde.

In fact, Signor Enea did say no, and Matilde was forced to intervene.

"Enea, you really do have to let us go upstairs to clean your study and workroom. I can just imagine the dust that must have built up. The wood stove must be full of ashes, and the books have probably absorbed so much soot that you can't even open them anymore."

"Mama," he replied, "please forget about my study. I'm the one who has to live in it, and I like living in it just the way it is." His blue eyes looked tired. "I'll take care of airing it out and getting rid of the dust."

Matilde was aware that he would not do it, but she did not feel like insisting too much. She lived through that period of time as if it were a passing phase, and she awaited the end of it without any desire to make change come more quickly.

Enea had resumed going out every morning at precisely a quarter past eight as if he had to go to work, but Matilde knew he had not shown up at Colamele's again. He came home for dinner, then almost always went up to the quarters above the lemon-tree room, and started to spend a good part of the night there once more too. When he was up there, he came downstairs a lot to go into the kitchen to pour himself something to drink or to make the usual trips to the bathroom near his bedroom. Afterward, he burrowed in again among his things.

Some evenings he went out around eleven o'clock, and always took his moped. He rode around a lot less now than in the past. When he let his mother know he intended to go out, Matilde prepared herself to stay awake and wait up for him, sitting either in her bed reading or in front of the television. She had discovered that some of the channels had programs running until late at night, and she kept herself company that way until she heard the gate squeak and the gravel crunch under the moped's tires.

George Lockridge had not set foot in the house again, and during that entire time Matilde only received a couple of phone calls. One was from Dono, who wanted to know how Enea was and seemed very worried when Matilde told him about the insatiable hunger that had come over her son the last few days. In fact, it was really a case of him gorging himself. Enea was coming and going from the refrigerator, munching away at all hours. He even carried around cookies and chocolate in his pocket.

"Try to get him to come see me," said Dono finally. "Polyphagia is a bad sign."

The second call was from Andreino Colamele. Once Matilde had overcome the initial moments of embarrassment over not having called him again, she was happy to have a chance to talk with him.

"Enea is recovering. Slowly, but he's recovering," she announced to him.

"Someone saw him walking around the city," replied Colamele, "but he hasn't even dropped by to see me. In fact, I was hoping to catch him at home to tell him a thing or two. I don't think I deserve this kind of indifference."

"It's not indifference, believe me. We were talking

about it just the other evening. It's that he can't decide what to do with his life. Dono insists that for a while Enea must not take on any steady commitments. He has to take care of the problems with his health first, but Enea's resisting it. He feels like getting back to work. You'll see, sooner or later you'll find him in your office when you're least expecting him."

"Sooner would be better than later," declared Colamele. "He can afford not to make decisions about his life, but I have to make decisions about my business. If he doesn't understand that work is the only cure for all ills, I'll hire one of those young men who don't have their heads in the clouds and are still full of fresh energy to take his place. In any case, ask him if I have to send his severance pay to the house or if he'll at least come in to pick it up himself."

"I'll tell him," murmured Matilde, falling prey to a discouraging sense of defeat.

Andreino Colamele paused before adding, "Between us, there's no need for a lot of explanations. You know I'm saying this with his best interests in mind. If Enea is willing to return, I'll be happy to take him back, if for no other reason than because we're used to working together and we understand each other. Besides, we may as well say it, I'm doing it a bit for you too. Anyhow, Enea was born to be behind a desk, solving problems that would appear insurmountable to other people. For certain things, he's the only one around. Tell him, the hardhead."

"I'll tell him," Matilde repeated.

∿

At that moment Enea was on via de' Renai sobbing uncontrollably, his hands clutching a small, white angora jacket that had belonged to Nanda. He had promised the young woman's mother that he would gather the things left in the apartment and bring them to her. When he realized how few things she had possessed, he was overcome with emotion. Two pairs of blue jeans, a few small sweaters that had lost their shape, an old synthetic fur coat, a skirt, a blouse, the red dressing gown, and a handful of underclothes. When he had happened to pick up the white jacket, which Nanda had never worn because the angora tickled her nose, he had sat down on the bed and started to cry, softly at first, and then in sobs that became more and more uncontrollable.

He had bought a large suitcase in a department store and when he placed the garments inside, folding them carefully, he realized it was not even half full. He went into the large shower stall, lifted the blue waffle-weave cotton bathrobe off the hook, took the hair brush, which still had some strands of blond hair between the bristles, and picked up the bar of soap from the floor. He looked at those things for a few seconds and then decided not to take them to Nanda's mother. He could not explain why, but he sensed that those things—the last ones she had used before her death—would have given her a particularly atrocious kind of pain.

When she had moved to via de' Renai, Nanda had arrived with a long, yellow-and-blue-striped acrylic bag, which was now empty, hanging on the rectangular coat rack attached to the wall behind the front door. Enea took it and put the bathrobe, the soap, and the brush inside, and then hung the bag back up.

He closed the suitcase and headed toward the door. Before leaving, he turned to look around the apartment.

Until that morning, nothing in the apartment had been touched, not even the two dirty plates covered with left-over eggs sitting in the sink or the open magazine lying on the red tile floor near the bed. Yet it did not seem as if Nanda would come back at any moment. The place had a definitively lifeless air about it, an air suggesting someone had died.

❧❧

"Hello. Please come in."

Nanda's mother welcomed Enea in her usual kind voice, whispering as if she were always afraid of waking someone up. When she saw the suitcase she did not even show a sign of taking it. She pointed at the floor, where he set it down before following her into the living room.

The table in the corner of the room was set for lunch with a cross-stitched white tablecloth on it, porcelain plates with a blue and gold border, and crystal goblets. The flatware was made of silver and arranged next to the plates with symmetry, each napkin was folded in a triangle.

"I hope you'd like to stay for lunch," said Nanda's mother, sitting down close to Enea on the couch. "My husband should be back any moment."

She had gone to the hairdresser and her face was more relaxed. She was wearing a pink flannel blouse with dainty embroidery on the collar and down the front and a pleated blue skirt that gave her an extremely youthful appearance. With her short brown hair done in soft waves and just a touch of gray-blue eyeliner around her eyes she looked very young. Enea estimated she must have been about forty, give or take a year. The realization filled him with dismay. Nanda's mother was younger than he, and her father probably was too.

Though at first he felt anguish over how old he was, immediately afterward he was totally elated about having been granted the experience of living beside Nanda.

24

The young man does not know what is happening. He only knows he has to escape.

Inside the orange tent, he had been in his woman's arms, protected as if in a womb one minute, then the next minute all hell broke loose.

They arrived from France a few days earlier for a peaceful vacation they had dreamed about for a long time. Now the dream is about to become a bloodbath. They had been kissing each other when a sharp rustle made him turn his head and pull his lips away from hers. Two eyes are staring at him through the round, transparent, plastic window at the back of the tent, when a long knife suddenly rips through the material.

The young man's fear spreads to the woman, who stiffens, and cranes her neck to see, following his eyes. Now the man's eyes have disappeared. Only the two torn strips of the tent remain, and the window, which is hanging awry, is held only by a small shred of cloth. The two strips lightly snap, blown by the wind.

The two young people stare at that opening that fills up with darkness, and the blackness of the night stands out against the orange tent. When the first shot explodes they are still turned in that direction, and they do not see the man who has slipped inside from the opposite end of the tent. He is so tall that he had to get down on his hands and knees to come in. The first bullet hits the young man in the arm, the next two, shot one right after the other, seem aimed at the same spot. The fourth bullet grazes his lip, splitting it open clear to the bottom of his nose. His mouth full of blood, the young man extricates his legs from the woman's, gets on his knees, and shakes his head, spurting large red spots onto the woman's body and the air mattress. He stretches out his legs and arms like a sprinter taking off, and flies outside, brushing against the torn strips of fabric. He rolls over on the grass, stands up, runs into the darkness. His ears are still thundering with the sound of the shots that come again and again, eight times in a single long thunderous rumble.

He loves the woman, but in that moment he is not thinking about her. He is not thinking about anything. A thicket of bushes appears suddenly in front of him. He runs into it, moves his outstretched hands, scratching his palms and arms. He tries to go around it, his memory guiding him mechanically to the left, where the bushes stop at the edge of the path.

When he turns, the man is standing in front of him, at least eight inches taller than he is, a huge black shadow that the young man barely makes out in the dim light shining through the tear in the tent onto the bushes.

He whirls around, and the knife plunges into his back, then is pulled out. The young man only feels a hard blow that takes his breath away. He thinks the man hit him with his fist, and he turns around to face him. This time the knife goes into his abdomen and tears his flesh, burning like fire. He opens his mouth to scream, but his cry is suffocated by the knife penetrating his carotid artery.

The young man gurgles something, and falls on the grass. Blood spurts on the shrubs, splattering them with red spots.

The man stands perfectly still to observe for a long moment. When he sees that the young man is not moving anymore, he takes a few uncertain steps toward three empty paint cans left against the trunk of a tree, along with some black plastic garbage bags. He drapes the bags over the body, as if to hide it, and then he puts the three cans on top of it, upside down.

He goes back to the tent. The woman is dead by then. Her face is disfigured from the three bullets that hit her in the head, and the left side of her chest is soaked in blood from a wound made by a fourth bullet. The man gets down on his knees at the opening of the tent, grabs the woman by her legs and pulls her toward him, moving slowly backward until the body is completely outside. He lays the big knife on the ground, takes out one that is thinner and sharper, and begins the patient operation of making the incisions, first around the left breast and then the pubis.

He mumbles softly while the big hands move skillfully, cutting, separating, and setting the trophies on the grass.

The man steps back from the body, looks it over and does not like what he sees in the bright orange light falling directly on the body from inside the tent. He lets out a long sigh, takes the woman by her ankles again, drags her up to the tent and then back inside, and lays her on top of the air mattress, leaving a long trail of blood behind him.

As he goes out, he carefully draws together the two flaps that close the entrance. Moving to the back of the tent, he does the same thing with the torn pieces of fabric, putting one piece over the other so that the plastic window will not dangle in the air.

Finally, he gathers his trophies and instruments of death and walks away, taking long, weary steps along the path that disappears in the countryside beyond the thicket of shrubs.

∽◦◦∾

"Enea! Enea, wake up!"

Matilde had come into her son's bedroom throwing open the door so violently that it slammed against the wall. Standing next to the bed, she was now shaking Enea, who was still immersed in a deep sleep. He opened his eyes, covering his head with his arms, grumbling for her to leave him in peace. Matilde did not give up and kept on shaking him and yelling at him to sit up because she had to talk to him. She stopped only when she saw him push his hands down on the mattress and slide his shoulders up the headboard into a sitting position.

"Why are you so upset" he grumbled, still sluggish, his head drooping. "I didn't shut my eyes until dawn."

"Where were you the other night?" repeated Matilde. Now that she was able to communicate with her son, she suddenly saw herself as an unrestrained Fury and forced herself to regain a reasonable tone. But her voice sounded strange all the same. "Try to remember."

Enea looked at her from under his swollen eyelids,

221

and had a difficult time grasping the meaning of her words and answering to the point. "I don't have the vaguest idea. I don't even know what day it is today."

"Today's Tuesday," said Matilde. "I'm talking about Friday."

"How do you think I can remember what I did on Friday? If I wasn't at home, I must have gone out and around somewhere. I probably met someone, and stopped to chat a while. Does it seem normal to you to wake me up like this to ask me where I was?" His voice had turned disgruntled.

"I know, I know," murmured Matilde. "To someone who has just woken up, it can sound crazy. But I've been up since six, and I listened to the early morning news on the radio."

"So?" asked Enea, who suddenly seemed totally awake.

"So they found two more bodies, up at Scopeti, just a little ways away from San Casciano, where your cousins live."

Matilde moved away from the bed, feeling more and more embarrassed about the way she had burst in. She took a few steps around the room, wringing her hands, her mouth tightly closed.

"Are you afraid the two bodies might be my cousins?" asked Enea. He had an ironic expression on his face now, bordering on pity.

"No, not even in my worst nightmare," replied Matilde. She stopped in front of the chest of drawers for a moment to look at her image in the cloudy mirror. She detested herself for the way she had lost control and for being unable to reason with a cool head. "It's that I worry," she said softly. "When you're out wandering around at night, I don't have any peace at all." She straightened the white doily on the pewter tray that held the bottle of insulin and two small syringes that were still sealed in the transparent paper. "You may think I'm crazy, but when I know you're out wandering around in the dark I can't help but connect your image with death."

Enea nodded in agreement, becoming serious again, and he came out with one of his strange replies. "You're right. Death is precisely what follows me around when I wander in the dark."

❧

". . . a gruesome discovery has come to light," said the man on the television screen. "On the same night as the double homicide, the killer sent a letter to a woman prosecutor in the city." A pause. "Inside the envelope was a fragment that was mistaken for a piece of marijuana at first. The prosecutor, in fact, has been working on investigations into the drug world for several months. In reality, the fragment was a piece of dried flesh from a female breast."

Matilde put her hands over her ears, thinking they should not broadcast such shocking news. She got up to go turn off the television, but stood with her hand held out, paralyzed by what the journalist was saying.

"The envelope was mailed from the same mailbox where the second twenty-two caliber bullet was found, either left or lost by the killer."

At this point Matilde shut off the television and turned around, certain that she had to search for something. She looked around, trying hard to remember what she had in mind when she had moved. A sentence spoken on the television had prompted her to glance around, but she could not remember precisely what it was. She went back in front of the television, stood staring at the blank screen, letting each word she had heard come back into her mind.

The twenty-two caliber bullet.

Now she knew.

Ever since the preceding homicide, Matilde had had some idea buried deep within that seemed as if it might surface now and then, yet was never able to jog itself completely free. She had not made any effort to understand exactly what caused the nagging prickle that tortured her thoughts whenever they spoke about bullets. Maybe, she told herself, without realizing it she had tried to protect herself from an inquiry that could be deeply painful for her. Now, however, it was clear what stirred up the uneasiness inside her, and she decided that if something had to be done, then it had to be done.

At dinner that evening she sensed that Enea would go out from the way he lingered in the dining room instead of going straight up to his study as he did when he was staying at home. Matilde let a plan of action take shape in her mind. She peeled an apple with methodical movements, and at the same time, as if her mind were suddenly freed of any snares, she studied every detail of the things she had to do.

She had kept the newspapers from the last few days, whose pages were full of articles on the murders of the couples. One of them in particular carried a piece of news again that (Matilde now knew) could be the solid proof Andreino Colamele had spoken about. She did not go so far as to think that she had intentionally repressed it until that moment in an attempt to avoid the inevitable. She was simply surprised that she had not thought of it sooner.

As soon as Enea had left, she went into the sitting room, took the pile of folded newspapers sitting on the étagère, and looked for the news item. She found it right away, in the first newspaper she read. The kind of bullets used by the murderer was almost impossible to find by now. They were called Winchester H, came from a lot made in Australia between 1952 and 1956, and had been imported in Italy between 1961 and 1965. Only a few of those bullets could still have been around.

She folded the newspaper up again, put it back with the others, and headed toward Nanni's study. Despite the fact that the windows were opened every morning, the room was permeated by a stuffy smell, made more pungent by the dust clinging to the spines of the books. Matilde knew where to look. She went over to the left door of the bookcase, opened it, and put her hand in the gaping space left between the volumes when Enea had moved some of them into his study. She moved her hand several times, from right to left, hitting up against the leather book covers, but she did not find anything. Then she remembered. The small boxes she was looking for had not been in the bookcase for a long time. Enea must have taken them upstairs during the days when he was selecting the books to use as his own and those to leave in the study on the first floor.

She did not want to go upstairs in the quarters over the lemon-tree room again. She felt acutely afraid at the thought of climbing all the way up there alone in the darkness of night. She knew that after this last inspection she would have faced the truth one way or another. She still hesitated for several minutes, but in the end she reminded herself that she had decided to finish her search, whatever the result might be. So it was that she went into the kitchen and took the brass ring with the two keys off the hook on the cupboard.

In the hallway, she only turned on the wall lamp in the corner. It gave off an extremely dim light because one of the two light bulbs had burned out and no one in the house had found the desire or the time to replace it yet. Matilde had asked Saveria to take care of it and also Enea, but they had not done anything about it. Now she was going down the long, hostile hallway in near darkness, walking stiffly as she took necessarily slow steps, headed toward her son's absolution, or solid proof of his guilt.

When she was in his study she turned on the floor lamp and went over to the table. She noticed that the room was unusually neat, with the shelves perfectly dusted, the pens and pencils placed in a pewter tankard. Books were still piled up on every piece of furniture, but in small, orderly piles. The papers were put away in light blue folders, labeled by hand in big, green block letters, indicating the contents. It was as if Enea had decided to leave nothing around him in disorder, sparing others the burden of reading and making a list of all those heaps of papers, in case someone might have had to go through his things. Matilde stood for a few minutes with her brow furrowed as she tried to make sense out of that strange behavior, and then she shook herself out of it.

She opened the top drawer on the left, giving it a tug to make it slide, and immediately saw the small gray boxes with the faded yellow label. They almost filled the entire bottom of the drawer. When she picked a few of them up, Matilde realized that some were empty and some were full. Nanni had bought them more than twenty years ago, coming home one

evening with a big box, which was also gray with a yellow label that covered the entire lid. He had boasted
about the features of those bullets. He and Enea had
even laughed about it and had planned to try them out
in the woods as soon as they went to Impruneta.

Matilde carried one of the small boxes over to the
light from the floor lamp and put on her glasses, which
she wore on a small chain around her neck. The first
letter of each word was printed in a floral type so intri-
cate that she had to reconstruct it after she read the letters following it.

Winchester H. Made in Australia.

She put the small box back with the others, carefully closed the drawer, and turned out the light.

25

"Should I prepare something for Signor Enea too?" asked Saveria, sticking her head in the door to the sitting room.

"Naturally," answered Matilde, without turning to look at her, and added, "Why do you ask?"

"Signor Enea didn't come home last night."

Matilde finished folding the newspaper back up, put it on the desk, and smoothed it out with both her hands. "Right, he didn't come home," she repeated softly. "Then don't bother. Bring me a cup of coffee and forget about setting the table."

When she heard Saveria's steps walking down the hall, she took the newspapers from the last few days that she had kept on the étagère and put them into two neat piles on the desk in front of the window, covering the one she had folded up first. She looked outside, beyond the oak tree's low, tangled branches toward the green hill and Fiesole. She had to force herself not to think.

"Here's the coffee," said Saveria.

When she realized that the top of the desk was covered, the woman went to set the tray down on the small table next to the television set.

Matilde slowly turned around, pointing out the newspapers to Saveria. "Take those away. They can be used for cleaning the windows. You can put them in the garage."

She poured her coffee, put in half a teaspoon of sugar and a drop of milk, and sipped it halfheartedly. It was not hot enough, but she did not notice. Enea had not come home the night before, and she was almost relieved. She would not have known how to face her son that morning.

When she had finished drinking her coffee, she went into her bedroom and opened the armoire to choose a jacket. She had to go out, but she did not feel like changing her clothes. She decided on a three-quarter length, blue cloth jacket. It would cover the light blue sweater she generally wore when she was staying home and the dark gray, vicuña wool skirt that had slightly lost its shape around the hips.

Matilde told Saveria she would be back soon. She walked along the path, taking slow steps, opened the gate, and went out onto the sidewalk. A distinguished woman, wearing sturdy, low-heeled shoes, her legs still slender, her hair neatly combed and swept back with small wavy curls around the nape of her neck.

When she went into the pharmacy the elderly clerk greeted her attentively. "Good day, Signora Monterispoli. We haven't seen you for a long time. Have you noticed what a beautiful spring we're having?"

"Yes, very beautiful," said Matilde. "Is the doctor in?"

"You know, for some time now he has been coming in only in the afternoon, even though I shouldn't say so. He doesn't feel like staying in the pharmacy the entire day anymore." The clerk was slender and distinguished looking. If it had not been for the fact that he did not have the medical cross on his white smock, he could have been taken for the pharmacist. He had worked there for twenty years, and he knew as much about it as a doctor.

"He's doing just the right thing," commented Matilde. "At a certain point in life one should pull the oars into the boat and relax. Do you have some rose water?"

"Certainly we do. The best, if I may say so." The clerk turned around to take a small blue bottle off one of the shelves. "Anything else?"

Matilde answered no, and then looked as if she were thinking it over again and added, "Since I'm already here, it would be better if I got my son's insulin. He only had one bottle left yesterday morning and I wouldn't want him to run out."

"He uses the semi-slow-acting, if I'm not mistaken," said the clerk, heading for the back of the pharmacy.

"No, no, the fast-acting," Matilde yelled after him.

The clerk came to a stop, uncertain, and then turned half way around. "You're sure about that? It seems to me he uses the semi-slow."

"In fact, he used to use that. But after the last tests Doctor Morigi prescribed the fast-acting insulin. Actrapid, I think he said."

The clerk pushed the button to make the shelves rotate, and when he saw what he was looking for, he picked up a small box and came back to the counter in front of Matilde. "Do you have the prescription, Signora Monterispoli?"

"Oh, no," replied Matilde. "My son has it. I thought I would pick it up for him because he's very busy these days and his head's somewhere else. I'm sure he would forget to buy it."

"Please remind him to bring the prescription when he comes in," said the clerk. "I couldn't give it to him without it, as you know."

"Don't worry, he'll bring it in the next time."

When she arrived at home, Matilde took off her jacket and hung it back up in the armoire. She unwrapped the packet with the rose water and the insulin, took the small bottle out of the box, and looked at the label. It was yellow, whereas the semi-slow had an orange one. She was uncertain for a moment, then she sighed and went into Enea's bedroom. Surprised, she stopped when she saw Enea's bed, which was still made. She had forgotten that her son had not come home the night before. She took a few steps toward the bed, uncertain again, and in the end she made up her mind to go over to the dresser. She took the insulin with the orange label and put the one she had just bought in its place, being careful to turn the bottle so that the label was facing the wall. She slipped the small bottle from the tray into her pocket, and then she went into the kitchen, where Saveria was cutting up the vegetables for that evening's soup. She did not feel like being alone.

"Will Signor Enea come home for dinner?" asked the woman. Her face was serious, and she stopped her quick strokes with the knife to give her mistress a questioning look.

"Let's hope so," answered Matilde, reaching out to pick up a handful of peas that she started to shell.

"What if he doesn't come home?"

The woman's worried face surprised Matilde, who

stopped to stare at her. "Why shouldn't he come home?" she asked.

Saveria shrugged her shoulders, starting to wield the knife on the cutting board. "Since I've been working here, he hasn't stayed out often at night."

"He must prefer not to come home," said Matilde so softly that Saveria could not understand. Then she added, "Signor Enea is a full-grown man. He ought to know what he's doing."

ﾍﾟﾍﾟ

As long as Saveria was in the house, Matilde managed to make the time pass one way or another, but when the maid left, she was counting the minutes with her forehead up against her bedroom window, her eyes glued to the path. For the first time, she regretted that she could not get in touch with George Lockridge. He could surely tell her where Enea was at that moment. But given the fact that the Englishman did not have a phone, Matilde would not know how to reach him.

When it was nine o'clock, she started to think that Enea would not come. She had waited for him for an hour, sitting in front of her plate crumbling a bread-stick between her fingers, and she was about to make up her mind to eat when she heard the gate squeak and his footsteps coming up to the house. She cleaned the crumbs off the tablecloth, wiping them away with one hand and catching them in her other palm, and then she dropped them on her plate.

"Sorry, Mama," said Enea, as he stuck his head in the door to the dining room. "I'm going to my bed-room for a minute and I'll be right back."

Matilde moved into the kitchen to pour the soup warming on the stove into the tureen. She carried it over to the table and sat down again. Several minutes went by before Enea joined her.

That evening, Matilde did not touch a bite of food and stared off into space for a long time. When she finally looked over at Enea, she saw that her son's forehead was bathed in sweat and he was fidgeting in his chair.

"Don't you feel well?" she managed to ask.

"I don't think so," he stammered. He shook his head back and forth, and his breathing was labored. "I had better go to bed."

Enea got up, supporting himself with the table, his hands gripping the edge, and it took him several seconds before he was able to turn and stagger over to the door. He misgauged the size of the opening and ran into the doorjamb, and he leaned against it with his face against the wood for another long minute. He finally let go and went out. His feet dragged along the runner that covered the hallway floor.

Then Matilde stood up too, hard as a rock. She poured herself half a glass of water and went into her sitting room, carefully closing the door. She went into her bedroom, closed that door too, walked over to the nightstand, and took the sleeping pill she had prepared that afternoon out of the drawer. She put it on her tongue and washed it down, drinking all of the water in the glass in one gulp.

Since she had an empty stomach, and during the short time she had resorted to sleeping pills she had always taken just half a pill, it took effect quickly.

She had just enough time to get ready for bed, slip between the sheets, and ask for God's forgiveness before she was already fast asleep.

ᑐᢦ

The next morning she woke up half an hour earlier than usual, her mind perfectly clear. She waited for Saveria to arrive and for the table to be set for breakfast, let some more time pass by, and then went into the kitchen and said to the woman, "We have to call Signor Enea."

"Why do you want to call him? He has always woken up on his own."

When Saveria did not want to do something, there was no way to make her budge.

"He's late this morning," said Matilde. "Besides, we need to quit warming up the milk and coffee all the time."

She knew it was up to her. It was clear in her mind what she would find in her son's room. She was very familiar with the signs of a diabetic coma. In fact, the bed was all messed up, the covers and sheets in a heap at the foot of the bed, the pillow on the floor as if it had been flung off by the strength of the convulsions. From the door, only Enea's legs could be seen on the mattress. The rest of his body had ended up on the floor, with his face lying flat on the rug, his arms spread wide open. The top of his pajamas had crept clear up to his shoulders, along with his undershirt, leaving his pale back uncovered.

Matilde closed her eyes for a moment, and when she opened them again she was already standing in front of the dresser. She pulled the bottle of insulin with the orange label out of the pocket of her wool jacket, exchanged it with the other one on the embroidered doily, and put the bottle with the yellow label in her pocket.

When she went out, she left the door open and went down the hall staggering slightly. She went into the kitchen, and Saveria knew from the look on her face that something very serious must have happened. Matilde moved her hand in the air, unable to say anything, and the woman went up to her, worried.

"Get a hold of my brother-in-law, at the hospital," Matilde managed to get out. "Tell him it's urgent . . . to come right away. My son is sick. . . . My son is dead."

❧✦❧

Dono Monterispoli arrived with Doctor Morigi. Seeing Matilde's expression was all he needed to decide that any questions would have been superfluous. He took his colleague by the elbow and led him toward Enea's bedroom. The two of them stayed there long enough to verify the death and to recompose the body on the bed. Then they joined Matilde in the living room, where she sat on a chair, her blue eyes glazed, and they sat down on the couch side by side.

"Unfortunately, what you feared was right, Matilde," murmured Dono. "Enea is dead." He cleared his throat, his voice having broken on the last word.

"You didn't hear anything last night?" asked Doctor Morigi. "He must have made quite a bit of noise with an attack like that."

"My room is on the other side of the hall," answered Matilde, pointing in the direction of her room. "Besides that, there's another room in between it and the hallway, and I keep both of the doors closed out of habit. Then, yesterday evening, as I've been doing for a while, I took a sleeping tablet."

Dono Monterispoli and Doctor Morigi admired her composure.

"You don't have to worry about a thing," said her brother-in-law after a brief silence. "I'll take care of everything. The certificates, the funeral service, the obituary."

Matilde suddenly turned her head. "The obituary? Are you sure you want to do the obituary? I'd prefer that the news were announced after the funeral."

"I know, pain is an extremely private emotion," replied her brother-in-law. "But even when tragedies occur, one has social obligations. Enea must have had friends who would be hurt if they weren't informed." He turned toward Doctor Morigi. "Will you take care of the death certificate?"

"Yes, certainly."

All three of them sat in silence, until Doctor Morigi decided he had to say something. He tried hard to find some words of comfort and looked at Matilde, saying softly, "Your son wasn't well at all lately. Maybe also because he was neglecting himself. He looked very tormented. Who knows, he may have found some peace. Who can say? He might have had to go through even worse pain otherwise."

He stopped, dissatisfied about the banality of his words, and was surprised to see that Matilde was staring at him with an intense look of unequivocal gratitude in her eyes.

26

The day of the funeral the sky was clear, and the sunshine made the outlines of the trees and spacious villas scattered on the hillside stand out more sharply. The windows of the Monterispoli house were closed, but the sun's rays beating against the panes warmed the rooms all the same.

Matilde was sitting in the living room, dressed in blue and wearing a string of pearls around her neck. She held her head high and gave a slight nod each time someone came in to offer their condolences. A lot of people had come, more than had been expected, and she was surprised that she felt pleased about it. After all, the Monterispoli name still had its own importance in the city.

Some polished, noiseless cars had dropped nurses and doctors from Santo Giovanni Hospital off at the gate. The people from the neighborhood had come on foot, with the women wearing hats and the men dressed in dark suits. The owners of the shops Matilde frequented were also there. Saveria came with her entire family, including her daughters-in-law and grandchildren. Before she changed her clothes in the small room near the kitchen, Saveria had prepared some

pitchers of milk and pots of coffee, and also some cookies and two cakes that she had brought from home. As
she arranged the cups and teaspoons on the large silver
trays, she was sobbing so hard that Matilde had to tell
her to get a hold of herself.

"How can you keep from crying, ma'am?" asked the
woman. "Now we're left all alone."

It was the comment that touched Matilde the most
out of all the things that had been said to her. She put
out her hand to pat her on the cheek, repeating, "Yes,
we're all alone."

As usual, Dono Monterispoli had risen to the occasion and had relieved her of all the worries. He had
chosen the type of funeral and the flowers to decorate
the church. Now he was the one receiving friends and
acquaintances in the portico in front of the house before inviting them inside to see Matilde. He managed
the people like a watchful policeman, keeping some of
them engaged in conversation outside until others had
emerged from the living room, and then admitted the
next group one at a time with elegant social graces. He
managed to be almost affectionate with Calambrina.
He gave an approving look at her classic suit, and held
her a moment in his arms, murmuring that it was a
comfort to see her.

When she saw Andreino Colamele standing in front
of her, Matilde looked him in the eye without saying a
thing, and he interpreted that silence as a reproach. He
sat down beside her, perched on a red satin ottoman,
and took her hand.

"Be brave, Matilde," he whispered. "Enea would
want you to be strong. I know you think I'm insensitive
because I kept insisting so much to make him come

back to work at my office. I was convinced it was the only solution. I couldn't imagine there was another solution, and such a dramatic one besides."

Matilde felt there was no need to reply, and so she continued to sit silently, her hand lying limp in Andreino's hands, until three people that she thought she had never seen before appeared in the doorway. A petite woman, who was slender and pretty, and a man with gray hair. Standing between them was a young man with brown hair who led them toward her.

They passed in front of her, first the older man, then the younger one, and then the woman, and softly voiced their pain over that tragedy. They had already started for the door when the woman came back. Paying no mind to Andreino Colamele, who was getting up to let her have the seat on the ottoman, she said, "I know how you feel, ma'am. I just lost a daughter, too. We parents deceive ourselves by thinking our children will remain ours forever. But the truth is that at a certain point they don't belong to us any more." She paused to shake her head before adding, "All that's left for us are tears."

Matilde leaned forward. "You knew Enea?"

"Yes, for a short time. He was a very good man."

I see, thought Matilde. All of the people who had been a part of her life and Enea's, even people whose existence she had never suspected, were there that day to remind her, each one in a different way, what her son had been.

In that instant George Lockridge came into her mind. George was not there. But she did not have time to give it any more thought, because Dono came into the room and walked over to the chair.

"We have to go, Matilde," he murmured, bending over her. "Are you sure you want to come all the way to the cemetery?"

Matilde nodded yes.

She lived through the service without realizing that the priest was giving the last farewell to Enea and that all the flower wreaths were for her son's death. She voiced the responses during the prayers and she stood up and sat down automatically according to the rules of the service. When four men dressed in undertaker's uniforms lifted up the coffin to take it down the aisle and outside, she was sorry there was not someone who was less of a stranger to shoulder that weight.

At the cemetery she suddenly came back to her senses. She watched the coffin as it was pushed into the wall of the family chapel, aware that Enea was gone forever. The picture of Nanni in the porcelain oval frame on the tombstone next to him seemed remote and estranged.

"How tall was this man?" one of the cemetery attendants muttered under his breath, as he kept pushing the coffin, which would not go all the way into the burial niche.

At that point, Matilde asked Dono to take her back home.

⟡

Matilde started to detest Saveria, who went on and on talking about Enea, stopping in front of her for half an hour here, half an hour there.

"They always said that if it rains on the day of a funeral, it means the dead person was good and the heavens are crying over his death," she mumbled one

240

morning. "If ever there were a good person in the world, it was Signor Enea. But it didn't rain that day."

"It's raining today," replied Matilde, listening to the showers that had been sweeping through the garden for hours. "A little late, but the heavens are crying over his death."

Another time, as soon as she went into the kitchen to put her coffee cup in the sink, Saveria stopped ironing and declared, "It's not up to me to say. It seems as if your mind's somewhere else though. So I'll remind you. When someone dies it's better to clean their clothes out of the closets and donate them to charity. The dead person can rest more peacefully."

Matilde reached the point she thought she could do without the woman. She could not bear someone referring to Enea as "the dead person."

It was always Saveria who brought it back to mind that sooner or later it would be necessary to go upstairs and put the quarters above the lemon-tree room in order, and she felt almost as if she would faint. She had not even gone into Enea's room again, but she knew the maid dusted in there every morning and opened the windows up wide. She had not even checked whether the bottle of insulin with the orange label was still on the white doily.

"He should've gotten married," said Saveria another day. "Signor Enea should've gotten married. At this moment you'd have grandchildren, who'd be a comfort in your life. A couple of beautiful little children running around the house are a blessing."

"Don't say such silly things," replied Matilde. "If Signor Enea had gotten married at the right age, at this moment his children would be men, busy in who knows what kind of work, quite the opposite of running around the house."

Several days later, the phone finally rang one evening, and Matilde was on the verge of not answering it. But the ringing did not stop, as if the person calling were sure she was there. So in the end she decided to pick up the receiver. It was George Lockridge. She recognized him immediately, by his shaking voice.

"Matilde, I just found out half an hour ago. I was in England. I made up my mind to go back to my own country for a few days." He had a fit of dry coughing. "I'd like to pay you a visit." As if he were afraid of being turned down, he quickly added, "I have something to give you. I think it belongs to you."

"Come whenever you want," Matilde answered. "I go out very rarely, if at all, these days. If you don't find me at home, just wait a few minutes. At most, I go as far as the newspaper stand."

"I'll come by tomorrow."

27

The day after George Lockridge's phone call, Matilde let the hours go by as she usually did now. She got up at half past seven and drank her coffee in the sitting room. (By then Saveria did not set the dining-room table for breakfast anymore.) She dusted the furniture in all of the rooms, except Enea's, drank a second cup of coffee, and after that she sat down with the newspaper in Nanni's study. Instead of reading it, she thumbed through the pages, skimming the headlines. Now and then her mind wandered, and she sat with the newspaper hanging in midair, staring into space.

For lunch she finished up the soup left over from the evening before and ate a small piece of cheese, just to make Saveria, who kept insisting she eat something, be quiet. Then she lay down on the bed as she had every day since Enea was gone. She could always doze at least an hour in the early afternoon, perhaps because the night was not long enough to wear off the effect of the sleeping pill she took every evening. When she got up she was no more rested than before, just a bit more fuzzy headed.

She waited for George Lockridge's visit without any curiosity, not even the slightest. She was happy to have a visitor, even if it was the Englishman, and she hoped he would come late in the day so that she would not be alone when darkness fell. She had started being afraid of twilight, when Saveria left and she was all alone in the silent house, the garden closing in upon her.

The doorbell rang. The sun was just starting to dip in the sky. She went to open the door, sure she knew who would be there. When she saw Andreino Colamele she was dumbstruck.

"Aren't you even going to invite me in?" asked the notary, cracking a smile that lacked any cheerfulness. He had a bouquet of wildflowers in his hand, which he held out to Matilde. "These are for Enea. If you go to the cemetery, take them to him on my behalf. Or else put them in front of his picture. I stopped going to cemeteries many years ago."

The sun was still hot and the air warm, so they decided to sit in the garden. Near the kitchen under an oak tree were four wrought iron chairs with thick cushions covering the seats and backs, and a round table with two pots of geraniums sitting on top.

"It's beautiful here," said the notary, lowering himself carefully onto one of the small chairs. He looked closely at Matilde, who was seated in front of him, and she seemed very sad, but her face was more relaxed than the last time. "How is it going?" he asked.

Matilde shrugged her shoulders. "How do you think it's going? I'm living with ghosts now." She no longer felt like feigning composure, as she had always done during the difficult times in her life. If her wounds burned, it was just as well that other people saw them burning too.

Andreino Colamele leaned toward her and patted her wrist. "Why don't you go away for a few days? The weather is so beautiful, and you're lucky enough to have that splendid house at Impruneta."

"I don't feel like it. I'm fine here. . . . Oh God, fine . . . so to say. Well, I'm used to it here."

Colamele felt a little embarrassed since Matilde just answered his questions without doing anything to keep the conversation going. He started to ramble about the Impruneta house, and let it slip that it was a pity to own an estate like that and not have any direct heirs to leave it to. Just as soon as he said it he wanted to bite his tongue.

Matilde stiffened, her mood becoming gloomy. "You can't have come to talk to me about wills."

"No, no, of course not," Andreino hastened to reply. "It's that when you've been a notary your whole life, as I have, certain things come into mind without you realizing it. Forgive me, if it sounded indelicate. I said it without thinking."

"In any case . . ." Matilde had never considered the question, but now it came naturally for her to say, "There are Nanni's nephews, the ones at San Casciano. They bear his same name, and they're orphans besides. I haven't seen them for several years, but that doesn't matter much." She paused, then added, surprised at the regret she felt, "They didn't even come to the funeral."

"Maybe they didn't know about it," Andreino consoled her, though he was not very convinced. "You know how young people are."

Matilde fell silent again, and Colamele wondered if it would not be better for him to leave, even though he had just gotten there. Matilde did not seem as if she felt like having company. Instead, she stood up, going towards the kitchen.

"I have some lemonade in the refrigerator," she said. "You still like lemonade, don't you?"

She came back carrying the crystal pitcher, glazed from the cold, and two glasses on an enameled tray. Andreino thought he would change the subject.

"Did you see?" he said. "They finally caught him."

"Who?" asked Matilde distractedly. She was concentrating on pouring the lemonade, and listened without really paying any attention. "Who did they catch?"

"The Monster. Red-handed, on top of it."

Matilde whirled around.

She looked at the wrinkles on the notary's face, his parchment colored skin, and his chapped lips. She turned her eyes toward a rose bush that was full of buds, and cast them back on Andreino. She did not say a word.

"The nightmare is finally over," he continued. "It seems they saved those young people by a hair's breadth. He had already pulled out his gun and was about to shoot through the car window."

"Who said so?" asked Matilde.

"They said so on the television, on the one o'clock news. The newspapers are putting out a special issue here in the city. All the people are out in the streets downtown. They even left their offices and they closed up the stores to celebrate."

"But are they sure it's him?" Matilde stared at the notary, every fiber in her body stock still, except for her lips.

"Of course they're sure. They caught him in the act, I'm telling you. There was this car with a young couple inside. There were police all around, hidden in the bushes. It's not certain yet, but maybe the couple was

246

two police officers. They might be the ones who opened fire first and wounded the man. Anyhow, they caught him, with a mean looking knife on him and his gun. He also confessed."

Now Matilde stared at a faraway point toward the hill of Fiesole. The skin on her face seemed transparent, as if all the blood had drained out.

"Now we can all rest easy," said Colamele. "You too."

Matilde gave a start, suddenly turning around to look at him. "Me? Why me?"

The notary hesitated a moment before he answered. "Because you're a part of the city too, and if certain things don't happen anymore it's better for everyone, isn't it?"

George Lockridge arrived just as Colamele was leaving. They met under the portico and barely greeted each other. The Englishman slightly bent his head, and Colamele quickly shook his hand, passing in front of him.

When they were alone, Matilde invited George to come in the house. "It's becoming damp out here," she said. "Besides, when darkness falls I can't stand being outside." Then she finally noticed the bulky bundle wrapped in newspaper that Lockridge was holding tightly in his hands. "Do you want to set that down somewhere?" she asked.

The Englishman shook his head. "No, no, I have to talk to you about it. Where should we sit?"

They went to sit on the couch in the living room. Once they were settled, Lockridge said, "Enea wanted to die. For a while he had been repeating that he wanted to die. And one way or another, he succeeded.

On the other hand, he had lost what I called his alibi to go on living."

Matilde looked at him. He was emaciated in the roomy red and green wool sweater, his fine hair falling down around his shoulders, his shortsighted eyes staring straight ahead. No reply came to mind because she did not understand what he could be talking about.

"How much do you know about Nanda?" asked the Englishman after a short while.

Matilde still did not understand. "I don't know anything about any Nanda," she answered. She would have liked to add that she preferred to remain in ignorance. Now each new discovery could only bring her more pain. George had already begun talking though, and told her about Enea and the young woman, the house on via de' Renai, how important the encounter with Nanda was for Enea and how he had suffered when she died.

"A few months ago," he concluded, lifting up the package that he had held in his lap until that moment, "Enea carved this bust. He gave it to her as a present one day at my house, but she didn't like it. She said it didn't look like her, and that, in fact, it brought bad luck. So it stayed at my house." The newspaper rustled while George unwrapped the head that Enea had carved.

Matilde saw the young woman with the empty eye sockets right in front of her eyes. The features had remained rough, and in comparison, the strands of hair appeared even more perfected and fine.

"Enea maintained that the more precise portraits are, the more they deceive," George explained with a sigh, as he looked at the sculpture too. "They can only capture you at a certain moment. The next moment

you're different, and so the representation of you becomes partial."

"Yet if they capture the soul," said Matilde automatically, "then the representation is complete."

The Englishman shook his head. "What you call the
soul can also change. And quickly. It depends on op-
portunities, and on what you happen to live through.
Take Enea, I'm sure that before he met Nanda he was
another person."

Lockridge ran his hand lightly over the head of the
young woman, as if he were caressing it. "He was so
precise and persistent with the hair, almost as if he
wanted to represent each strand one by one, that I
asked him what drove him to work like that. He answered that the strands of hair can change color but always remain true to themselves. In their own way they
reflect what a person is."

He got up, hesitating, and while he looked around
he did not stop talking. "Just think that to carve those
strands of hair he used I don't know what kind of scalpels anymore. They had the only blades that were sharp
enough."

He held the wooden head with extreme care as he
carried it over to the corner cabinet standing between
two windows to set it down, next to a blue porcelain
vase.

Matilde went over to close the window. When the
sun moved low on the horizon, the lime tree, whose
branches spread from that part of the house across the
entire corner of the garden, completely blocked the sky,
hastening the arrival of darkness in the living room.

"It's right for you to have it," continued George.
"You'll keep each other company."

❧❧ ❧❧ ❧❧ ❧❧ ❧❧

"Won't you sit down?" asked Matilde, anxiously. She did not want the Englishman to leave, she did not want to be left alone.

"No, I have to run. I'll come back another time."

Matilde walked along with him down the hall and to the portico, and stood next to the low wall until he had reached the gate and turned to look at her. Then she raised her hand in a weary wave goodbye, went back into the house, and closed the door.